"You're Afraid It Will Tarnish Your Sterling Political Reputation If Word Gets Out That You're Having An Out-Of-Wedlock Child!"

Kayla accused.

Tension and strength vibrating through him, Matt pulled her into his arms. Kayla felt his taut virile power and gazed up at him with wide hazel eyes.

"Don't be surprised," he murmured huskily. "Just thinking about you makes me burn."

Kayla stood passively in the circle of his arms for as long as her willpower held. Slowly, in sexy feminine response, she slid her arms around his neck and pulled him closer.

"It's such a risk," she murmured feverishly.

"You've already taken it," Matt soothed. "The baby is a reality now."

He thought she was talking about lovemaking, but she wasn't. She'd meant that loving was a risk. Did she dare to take it?

Dear Reader:

Welcome to Silhouette Desire – provocative, compelling, contemporary love stories written by and for today's woman. These are stories to treasure.

Each and every Silhouette Desire is a wonderful romance in which the emotional and the sensual go hand in hand. When you open a Desire, you enter a whole new world – a world that has, naturally, a perfect hero just waiting to whisk you away! A Silhouette Desire can be light-hearted or serious, but it will always be satisfying.

We hope you enjoy this Desire today – and will go on to enjoy many more.

Please write to us:

Jane Nicholls
Silhouette Books
PO Box 236
Thornton Road
Croydon
Surrey
CR9 3RU

BARBARA BOSWELL
DOUBLE TROUBLE

Silhouette Desire

**Originally Published by Silhouette Books
a division of
Harlequin Enterprises Ltd.**

First published in Great Britain in 1993
by Silhouette Books, Eton House, 18-24 Paradise Road,
Richmond, Surrey TW9 1SR

© Barbara Boswell 1992

Silhouette, Silhouette Desire and Colophon are
Trade Marks of Harlequin Enterprises B.V.

ISBN 0 373 58774 0

22-9304

Made and printed in Great Britain

BARBARA BOSWELL

loves writing about families. "I guess family has been a big influence on my writing," she says. "I particularly enjoy writing about how my characters' family relationships affect them."

When Barbara isn't writing or reading, she's spending time with her *own* family—her husband, three daughters and three cats, whom she concedes are the true bosses of their home! She has lived in Europe, but now makes her home in Pennsylvania. She collects miniatures and holiday ornaments, tries to avoid exercise and has somehow found the time to write six Silhouette Desires.

Other Silhouette Books by Barbara Boswell

Silhouette Desire

Rule Breaker
Another Whirlwind Courtship
The Bridal Price
The Baby Track
License To Love

Prologue

"**K**ayla, please! All you have to do is go to the dinner tonight and pretend to be me for a few hours. There's absolutely no chance that anyone will suspect a thing. Nobody who's going to be there even knows that I have a twin. Kayla, if you do this for me, I promise never to ask you for anything again."

Kayla McClure stared at her twin sister's flushed face. Looking at Kristina was like looking into a mirror. Their features were identical: large hazel eyes fringed by dark lashes, slightly upturned noses and wide, generous mouths. Even their hairstyles were similar, with long thick light-brown curls flowing over their shoulders. Right now, Kristina's jaw was set and her eyes glittered with a determination that Kayla knew well.

Kayla sighed. When she'd arrived from her home in Washington, D.C., to visit her twin in Harrisburg, Pennsylvania this weekend, she hadn't expected anything but a quiet sisterly visit. Kristina, it seemed, had a different agenda.

"Kristina, I want you to ask me to help whenever you need it, but when it comes to masquerading as you tonight, well, forget it. Twin-switching was cute in grade school and fun in junior high, but the few times we tried it after that were unmitigated disasters. I vowed never again. We're twenty-eight, Kristina, not eight," Kayla added reprovingly.

"Kayla, let me explain why I need this favor so desperately." Kristina bit at her thumbnail, a nervous habit she'd been fighting to break since childhood. "Boyd Sawyer called me yesterday. He's in Philadelphia—he presented some paper to a medical group—and he wants to see me tonight. He's flying back to Atlanta tomorrow afternoon so if I don't see him tonight..." Kristina's voice trailed off and she looked at the ground.

When she raised her head, Kayla saw that her sister's eyes were filled with tears. "I made such a mess of it with Boyd, Kayla," Kristina whispered. "It's all my fault that we broke up. I've been regretting it—and missing him—for the past two years."

Though Kristina had never confided the particulars of her breakup with Boyd Sawyer, Kayla knew how deeply in love her sister had been with the handsome, hardworking research physician. Kristina had been on the verge of hysteria the night she'd called Kayla to tell her that the romance was over. Boyd was taking a new job and moving to Atlanta. "It's all my fault," Kristina had said then, just as she continued to maintain now, two years later.

"I have to see Boyd, Kayla," Kristina said, her voice husky with urgency. "I have to! But, unfortunately, I'm also committed to attending this stupid fund-raising dinner tonight. If there were anyone else from the trade association available to attend, I'd arrange for it but there isn't. I have to show up."

"In other words, you have to be in two places at the same time tonight."

"With your cooperation, it can be done, Kayla," Kristina said eagerly. "If the real me is in Philadelphia with Boyd and you're at the dinner here in Harrisburg pretending to be me, I really can be in two places at the same time!"

Kayla felt her resolve weakening. What if she were to impersonate Kristina this one time? Would that really be so bad? Kayla grimaced. She knew the answers to those questions, of course, but this was no time for common sense. Swapping identities didn't allow for it. "Who is the fundraiser for?" she asked resignedly.

"A state senator from the Johnstown area. His name is Matt Minteer," Kristina told her. "He is his party's unanimous choice to fill the seat of an ancient congressman who is finally retiring from the U.S. House of Representatives. In that area of the state, the party's endorsement is tantamount to being elected. Minteer is kicking off his campaign tonight with the fund-raising dinner and all his party's important state politicians will be there along with a big contingent of lobbyists, of course."

"Of course," Kayla repeated, amused in spite of herself. She knew very well that wherever politicians gathered, the presence of lobbyists was a given. And Kristina was a lobbyist. "So I guess I'm a lobbyist tonight," Kayla said wryly. If attending a political fund-raising dinner while masquerading as her twin could benefit her sister's future happiness, it was worth the aggravation. Wasn't it? Once again Kayla firmly suppressed the niggling doubts assailing her.

"You're going!" Kristina shrieked joyfully and wrapped Kayla in a bear hug. "Oh, thank you, Kayla! Thank you!"

One

Kristina's jubilant thanks gave Kayla the impetus to ignore the nagging voice in her head that kept repeating one of their stepmother Penny's favorite axioms: "No good deed goes unpunished." She tried to think of another, more positive maxim as she arrived at the downtown Hilton Hotel shortly before seven that evening. Something about good deeds being their own reward, perhaps?

A sizable crowd was already gathered in the well-appointed ballroom. Fortunately, name tags were de rigueur and Kayla plastered one to her oyster-colored suit jacket, identifying her as Kristina McClure, PITA, an acronym for Pennsylvania Independent Telephone Association.

People approached her to chat. Kayla read their name tags and pretended that she knew them. The only conversation required in the noisy, jostling crowded room were the most superficial comments and responses, and Kayla had no trouble faking it. She was certain that nobody suspected an impostor in their midst.

A waiter came by, taking orders for drinks from the open bar. When Kayla declined to have one, he offered to fetch her a glass of fruit punch instead. She accepted gratefully and continued her conversation with Don Exner, a balding, middle-aged lobbyist who'd been chatting genially with her as "Kristina," of course.

And then, "Say, there's Matt now," exclaimed Exner. "Matt!" he called.

Kayla suppressed a groan. It was unfortunate that she happened to be standing with Don Exner when Matt Minteer happened along. But Kristina had assured her that she'd only met State Senator Minteer twice before and always in the company of others, so it shouldn't be too hard to fake the acquaintanceship.

The crowd seemed to part to make way for the tall, rugged figure. Kayla stood stock-still and stared. The towering man striding toward them seemed to have cornered the market on charisma. He fairly radiated that intangible quality, a priceless asset for a politician. And for a man.

Kayla gulped. Matt Minteer had also been blessed with an abundance of masculine good looks. He was very tall, about six foot three, and his strong muscular frame was pure masculine virility dressed for success in a navy suit. He had a shock of thick black hair and his eyes, a deep dark blue, gleamed with alert intelligence. His smile, easy and open with perfect white teeth and firm sensual lips, emanated friendliness and a kind of insistent sincerity that was invaluable to a political candidate.

At that moment, Matt Minteer joined her and Don Exner. The lobbyist grabbed the younger man's hand and shook it enthusiastically. "Matt, good to see you! Great turnout tonight. A real tribute to you."

"Glad you could make it, Don," Matt replied. His gaze went beyond the lobbyist and connected with Kayla's. A disconcerting hot streak raced through her.

"Hello there, Kristina," Matt Minteer said in a deep resonant voice that had an embarrassingly potent effect upon her. Kayla automatically took the big strong hand that he offered her to shake. The warmth of his fingers, the strength of his grip sent her reeling. She wracked her fogged brain for something clever to say.

Alas, all she could come up with was a lame, "It's nice to see you, Senator Minteer." Hardly original, definitely not memorable. If she'd deliberately chosen to be boring and bland, she couldn't have been more successful. Kayla winced.

Caught up in her own misgivings, Kayla was unaware that Matt Minteer was experiencing some definite discomfort of his own.

He tore his gaze from her alluring hazel eyes to her name tag. Kristina McClure, PITA, it said, just as he'd known it would. He didn't need a name tag to identify her. Gifted with a phenomenal memory for names and faces, he was able to remember everyone he'd ever met. It was an invaluable natural blessing for a politician, one that all the memory tricks or practiced word-associations could never replicate.

He recalled having met Kristina McClure before, but he knew he hadn't experienced this fierce spasm of desire now spiraling through him at the sight of her. Certainly he'd never felt this stunning and extremely inopportune surge of heat in his loins before, when he'd taken her hand in his.

Don Exner's impatient sniff penetrated the strange, private cocoon enshrouding the couple. Exner was miffed that the senator was giving so much time and attention to another lobbyist. Both Kayla and Matt suddenly realized that they were still holding hands. They quickly sprang apart, looking like a pair of guilty schoolkids confronted with their misdeed by the principal.

Then one of those obsequious waiters appeared, and Matt was glad of the diversion. "Sir, may I get you something to drink?"

"I'll have a beer," he said distractedly.

"Very good, sir." The waiter hurried off.

"A beer?" Kayla echoed, without thinking. She was accustomed to the sophisticated and rarefied atmosphere of D.C. politics where one's choice of drinks almost amounted to a political stand. Beer was not the statement that trendy, on-the-rise politicos aspired to make.

"Hey, Matt, at a top-drawer gathering like this, you're supposed to ask for something fancy. You know, like a frozen fruit daiquiri," Don Exner said jovially. "Think you could get one of those concoctions at Minteer's Tavern?"

"You have a choice of drinks at Minteer's Tavern," Matt replied dryly. "Beer, or a shot of whiskey or a shot-and-a-beer. Don't ask for anything else because if the bartender doesn't evict you, the rest of the patrons will."

He turned to Kayla. "I don't know if you've ever been to Johnstown, Kristina, but Minteer's Tavern is sort of a legend there. As famous as the Johnstown Flood, my grandfather likes to brag. Local lore has it that the original Minteer's Tavern was swept along in the flood waters back in 1889 but the patrons kept right on drinking and the bartender went right on serving until they washed up on the banks of the Ohio River in Pittsburgh, seventy-five miles to the west."

It was obviously a tall tale and an oft-repeated one at that. Kayla didn't know why she found it so funny, but suddenly, she simply couldn't stop laughing.

Matt was laughing, too. The sight of Kristina McClure tonight had bowled him over, but her laughter and her animation knocked him out. Her laughter wasn't forced, he could tell. Nobody but a skilled actor could fake the spasms of laughter that were shaking her.

She thought he was funny; he'd made her laugh. Matt was delighted. In the Minteer family, his younger brother John was known as the great raconteur whose comedic timing and delivery unfailingly produced genuine belly laughs. Matt was considered too serious and intense to be funny. And though he did try to insert a few humorous little asides in his speeches to liven them up, they usually ended up sounding urgent and earnest, a cause for concern, not fun. At best, his comic efforts might produce a smile or polite chuckle.

Exactly the sort of sound Don Exner had emitted at his tavern-in-the-flood tale. The older man's puzzled grin at the couple's continued hilarity soon turned into an irritated grimace. Finally, he murmured a polite excuse and drifted away.

Kayla and Matt exchanged dismayed glances. "Oh dear!" Kayla tried valiantly to pull herself together. "I didn't mean to exclude him but I was so tickled by your funny story."

Tickled. Matt felt another frisson of heat surge through him. Just hearing the word make him want to act on it. To start tickling Kristina McClure. To touch her. He recognized a startling, powerful urge to become very physical with her.

What was going on with him? he wondered, a little frantically. She was a lobbyist! He didn't interact with lobbyists except in the most professionally correct way. Yet tonight with Kristina McClure, he had a perverse desire for immediate, intimate interaction.

"I, uh, I'm glad you enjoyed it," he murmured. He should move away from her, right now! By spending so much time with her, he was running the risk of slighting the other lobbyists who would not appreciate someone else having such exclusive access to him. And then there was the other, more dangerous risk she presented—the shattering, sexual, and extremely inconvenient effect she was having upon him.

But he couldn't seem to make himself take the necessary steps to leave. Instead, he found himself scrounging around his mind for conversation. "So what's new with PITA?" he heard himself ask and instantly suppressed the urge to groan aloud. Using a political approach to open a conversation made him realize he'd been without a social life for too long.

Kayla froze. He couldn't have asked her a more unnerving question. Her knowledge of PITA affairs could be written on a postage stamp. "Well, we're still the independent phone companies," she said, striving for a humorous note to disguise her lack of facts. "We're still not AT&T."

To her relief Matt laughed appreciatively. "I'll keep that in mind." It appeared that he didn't want to talk shop, after all.

And then the waiter returned, handing Matt a tall, foaming beer and Kayla another glass of fruit punch. They thanked him and sipped their drinks. Once again, it became imperative to talk or to move on. This time Kayla took the conversational initiative. "Are you looking forward to changing your base of operations from Harrisburg to Washington?"

"My base of operations will always be the district that elects me," Matt replied at once. "Whether I'm serving in the Pennsylvania state senate or the U.S. Congress, my intentions and my priorities will always focus on my constituents."

"Oh, that's good!" Kayla said admiringly. "Very good. You didn't even miss a beat. And nothing pleases voters more than the notion that the candidate is theirs and eager to serve them."

Matt's smile dissolved. "You sound like one of those creepy political handlers who makes a living reinventing people who run for office."

Uh-oh. Kayla tensed. "You don't approve of hiring media consultants or political handlers? They can be quite effective and helpful to both candidates and elected officials," she added nervously.

She should know; she was one, though she hoped she didn't qualify as "creepy." Nor did she "reinvent" people. The way she saw it, she helped qualified candidates enhance their natural assets and assisted them in how to best present their message to the voters. And since opening her own consulting agency two years ago, she had steadfastly refused to take on anyone she wouldn't vote for, regardless of the financial incentive.

"What an image consultant actually does is make a pile of money giving lessons on how to hoodwink the public," Matt countered scornfully. "I hold that slick army of consultants, pollsters and media advisers largely responsible for the mess politics is in today. Voters don't trust their elected officials and no wonder, with those money-grubbing charlatans turning candidates into unctuous, media-slick phonies who are all form and no substance."

"I agree with you on some points," Kayla said quietly. She'd left the well-known wizardry of Dillon and Ward Consulting Associates because she was disillusioned and disgusted by their lack of ethics. In her own agency she could provide a service without chicanery.

"You should agree with me on every point when it comes to opposing those slick vultures." Matt wasn't ready to let the subject drop. Like all Minteers, he enjoyed a good argument and was just revving up. "Let's dissect what I said earlier. If, as you said, I didn't miss a beat, it's not because I've been rehearsing some pretty words written for me by a smooth operator with a degree in marketing and a feel for advertising. It's because I know my own mind and I speak it. And I also know my priorities, which are exactly that—priorities—not crowd-pleasing notions."

"If there were more politicians like you, the so-called image consultants would cease to exist," Kayla said wryly.

"And what a blessing that would be!"

"Then again, the most unflinchingly frank politicians often end up needing a media consultant more than anyone else," Kayla couldn't resist pointing out to him. "These days, no one in public life can afford to be too outspoken. You've been in a relatively sheltered political climate—a favorite native son in the majority party in local and state politics. Things change on the national level. It's entirely different."

"Honey, I could be running for president and I still wouldn't hire a media guru."

Kayla's eyes widened in horror. "Never, never call a woman 'honey.' It's practically instant political death."

"I wasn't being sexist." Matt scowled. "I was being . . . ironic."

"You're too blunt to be ironic. Anyway, irony is difficult to convey. It usually doesn't work in print and can be misinterpreted on the air."

"So if you were an image consultant, you'd steer your clients away from irony and outspokenness?" Matt shook his head. "Maybe you'd better stick to lobbying for PITA, Kristina. Your image and media advice is pretty lame."

Kayla thought of her paying clients; if they shared Matt Minteer's opinion, her business would be pretty lame. Which wasn't the case at all; she was making a comfortable living in a field that fascinated her. And she had the strangest need to share some of that with this disapproving stranger, Matt Minteer.

"Before you write off media consultants altogether, consider this," she injected earnestly. "Political neophytes need advice on how to break the deadlock of incumbency, and a consultant can provide honest assistance there. Sometimes newcomers need to bone up on such basics as grammar and diction and the fine points of etiquette, and a good media coach can provide—''

''Media coach!'' Matt hooted. ''Give me a break! Coaches are for football or basketball or hockey teams.''

''But the same principle applies,'' argued Kayla. ''Media coaches give guidance and instruction, just like coaches do for sports teams. Not everyone is born knowing how to act, dress and talk before the cameras.''

Matt shrugged. ''All you have to do is to be yourself on and off camera,'' he said simply. ''What's so hard about that?''

Kayla regarded him with a mixture of exasperation and awe. He was clearly a natural, whose honesty and self-confidence precluded the need for ''coaching.'' How did she explain that there were others, well-intentioned but less confident, inspired but not inspiring, who really did need extra help? It seemed futile, so she tried another tack. For reasons she didn't stop to ponder, it was imperative that she convince him that she was not creepy, slick or greedy.

''A good, independent consultant can also keep incumbent politicians from becoming too complacent and out of touch with their constituency. Sometimes, the consultant is the only one who dares speak the truth to politicians who are surrounded by sycophants who 'yes' them to death.''

''Politicians are not always surrounded by fawning yes-men,'' Matt protested. ''I won't tolerate anyone on my staff who doesn't have the guts or the brains to disagree with me.''

''Then you're an exception to the rule. To be honest with you, my opinion of most politicians mirrors yours of image consultants. But unlike you, I, at least, will acknowledge that there are exceptions.''

Matt arched his dark brows. ''You're very outspoken. I'm accustomed to schmoozing and smooth smiles from lobbyists, not straight talk.''

Kayla shifted uncomfortably. "So you don't approve of political consultants *or* lobbyists?"

Matt frowned at the edge in her voice and blamed himself for it. Couldn't he hold a simple conversation with an attractive woman without sounding off on something? His younger sister Anne Marie's voice echoed suddenly in his head: "Lighten up, Matt. Can't you make small talk without delivering a lecture on good and evil, according to the gospel of Saint Matthew Minteer?"

His eyes swept over Kristina McClure. Her beautiful, appealing smile had faded. He wondered if it was too late to make amends, then decided to try anyway.

He smiled at her, the famous Minteer smile, which effortlessly won both hearts and votes. "Let's bury the hatchet and move on to something else. Like what a maverick politician and a straight-shooting lobbyist can find to agree upon."

"That has a Wild West ring to it," Kayla said dryly. "Odd choice of metaphor for a Pennsylvania politician."

"You think I should work in something about iron and coke and coal and steel?" He was pleased that she was smiling again. And though he was aware that their dialogue bordered on flirting—*flirting!* at a political event!—he couldn't resist taking the next logical step.

"How do you feel about dessert? Not as a metaphor, the real thing," he added quickly. "Let's skip the dessert they'll be serving here tonight—it's a tasteless rubbery pudding falsely labeled chocolate mousse, an insult to both chocolate lovers and mousse lovers everywhere. We'll go over to Rillo's for some of their homemade ice cream. How about it, Kristina?"

He was asking her out! Kayla didn't hesitate for a moment. "I'd love to."

Later, she could fret about the foolish chance she was taking, going out with a politician while she was in the guise of Kristina. And not just any politician, but one who condemned her livelihood. But for now she was acting on impulse—a rarity for her—and loving it.

"Come up to the head table as soon as the speeches are finished," said Matt. His deep blue eyes were gleaming. "Then we'll steal away."

Kayla felt giddy. He made it sound so darkly exciting, as if they were headed for a secret, romantic rendezvous rather than simply going out for ice cream. "Yes," she said huskily.

He caught his breath, she caught hers and they gazed into each other's eyes for a long moment before the retiring congressman approached Matt and enjoined him to take his seat at the head table.

Matt turned his head once as he and the congressman made their way through the crowd. He saw that she was still watching him. She looked as dazed and dazzled as he was, and he felt immensely gratified that the attraction was mutual. He smiled, and even though she was halfway across the room from him, she smiled, too. An intimate, answering smile that connected them and promised so much.

Kayla felt a warm sweet glow stirring within her. She felt lighthearted and sensual and free, so far removed from her normal self that the everyday Kayla—that practical working grind—would have been suspicious of the sudden strange transformation.

But she was a different person tonight, a playful, happy Kayla who could think of nothing but Matt Minteer. Why, she was in love, Kayla decided as she sipped the white wine the waiter had just poured into her glass. Though she thought it happened only in songs, movies and books, it had happened to her. She had fallen in love at first sight.

And from the smoldering, sexy looks Matt kept sending her way, she was deliciously certain that he had fallen for her, too.

Two

"I've never had such a good time at a political fund-raiser," Kayla exclaimed to her nine dinner partners seated at the circular table. Though they had all been strangers when they'd sat down to dinner—only two had even a nodding acquaintance with Kristina—by the time the bad dessert was being served, Kayla felt as if they were all longtime friends.

During dinner they exchanged jokes, quips and stories, responding to even the most feeble attempts at humor with roars of appreciative laughter. And their table wasn't the only one to erupt with periodic bursts of hilarity throughout the evening. Everybody appeared to be having a wonderful time. Laughter and conviviality pervaded the ballroom, erasing inhibitions and enveloping them all in a happy glow.

It seemed perfectly natural when everybody at one of the tables began to sing, despite the absence of a band. Who needed instrumental accompaniment on a night like this? It wasn't long before everybody was singing, including the powers-that-be at the head table. If some didn't know the words, it didn't seem to matter. People simply made up their own lyrics. Kayla's table joined in the songfest and she was right with them, singing vigorously along to a fractured medley of show tunes.

When the waiter served the dessert, a glutinous concoction bearing a poor resemblance to any chocolate mousse she'd ever seen, she grinned, remembering Matt's description. And his invitation.

"I'm passing on this," she announced, pushing the dish aside. "I was invited to have dessert later at . . . at . . ." She couldn't remember exactly where. "Some place that serves homemade ice cream."

Her dinner companions laughed uproariously. At this point, any time that anyone said anything at all, the instantaneous response was peals of laughter.

"Going out for ice cream, hmm? Sounds like a hot date to me," said a jolly, fortyish, state representative from central Pennsylvania. "Who's the lucky guy, Kristina?"

A hot date for ice cream? Kayla chuckled, amused. But they'd all become such good pals, even if they did call her by her sister's name she saw no reason not to confide the "lucky guy's" identity. She playfully inclined her head toward the head table. "He's up there," she told them.

"Since all the men but one sitting at that table are very much married, you must be going out with the lone bachelor of the group," said another lobbyist, a young woman about her age. "Matt?"

"Minteer?" echoed the man across the table from Kayla. "That Matt?"

"That Matt," affirmed Kayla, sending the entire table into gales of laughter over the rhyme.

"I don't believe you," teased one of the state representatives. "Minteer doesn't date lobbyists. If you're really his date, prove it. Go up to him and sit on his lap." A loud dispute immediately broke out among her companions. Half believed Kayla, the other half insisted she should prove her claim. Kayla was in such a good mood, she decided to indulge them.

"I'll go over to his table to say hello but I won't sit on his lap," she said, rising to her feet. Strangely, the room seemed to lurch and she swayed, clutching the edge of the table for support. "For a moment there I felt as if I were drunk," she murmured, shaking her head. "But that's impossible. I've only had one glass of wine."

"You had at least two or three glasses of water, though," observed the person sitting next to her. "Gotta watch that stuff."

Again, everyone laughed heartily and Kayla trekked off, amid smiles and cheers. It didn't occur to her to feel shy or unwelcome at the head table. Everybody in this room was so friendly that Kayla felt at home with them all.

Her reception at the head table was welcoming. "Hello, beautiful lady," chirped the state party chairman. "Would you like to join us?"

Matt rose to his feet as Kayla approached him. His heart was pounding, and he felt as eager and taut with anticipation as a boy picking up his dream date for the prom. Taking both her hands in his felt perfectly natural to him. "Hello again," he said softly.

She smiled warmly, her heart in her eyes. "Hi." They gazed raptly at each other. Another round of singing broke out and Kayla chuckled. "You know, usually these political affairs are deadly dull but this is the most fun I've had in ages."

"Hey, we Pennsylvanians know how to party," boasted the lieutenant governor and the rest of the people at the head table cheered their agreement.

"I guess I'd better go back to my table now," Kayla told Matt. "Some of my friends didn't believe that you and I are going out for dessert tonight and asked me to prove it by coming over to your table and talking to you. A few wanted even more definitive proof.''

She giddily confided their dare. To sit on Matt Minteer's lap.

Right then and there, Matt audaciously accepted the dare for her. He sat down on his chair and pulled Kayla onto his lap. There was an approving roar from Kayla's table that spread throughout the ballroom. Matt linked his arms loosely around her waist. ''Now everybody in the place knows that you're my girl,'' he said, his blue eyes darkening possessively.

''Woman,'' she corrected automatically. ''It's politically incorrect to refer to females over the age of eighteen as girls.'' A male politician could be excoriated for that lapse; it was a lesson she immediately taught her new clients and continually stressed to the ones who had used her consulting service for a longer period of time.

''Whatever,'' Matt growled. At this moment, he was incapable of appreciating the benefits of her tutoring. He was too occupied with appreciating her, warm and soft and feminine on his lap.

Unable to resist, he moved one hand slowly upward to rest on her rib cage, just below the underside of her breast. With subtle fingertips, he could feel the provocative feminine swell. If she were to shift just a little, the whole soft weight of her would be in his hand. The desire to close that small distance between them—to cup and caress her breast, to take her soft ripe mouth in a kiss that was as hard and hungry as his body—was almost overwhelming.

Matt was vaguely aware that he was behaving in a manner most unlike himself. In public, he was impeccably proper in the presence of women. ''You're too stiff—why won't you loosen up?'' had been the constant disapproving refrain of his ex-almost-fiancée, Debra Wheeler.

Debra had been committed to spontaneous public displays of affection while his own deep natural reserve, coupled with his reluctance to expose himself and his partner to the attention such behavior would elicit, kept him firmly reined in when an audience was present.

It crossed Matt's bemused mind that if Debra could see him now, holding Kristina McClure on his lap at this all-star political fest, she would think that he'd been bewitched. Or that he was drunk. But he knew that was impossible. He'd had only one beer and one glass of wine, not enough to even give him a buzz. He certainly wasn't stupid enough to get drunk on a night like this.

Not that he ever drank himself into a state of intoxication. His Great-Uncle Arch's prodigious capacity for drink was known to every member of the family along with old Uncle Arch's well-documented trips to the hospital emergency room for injuries acquired in falls from bar stools, fistfights and a host of accidents. With an example like that, there were no hard drinkers among the younger generation of Minteers.

So if he wasn't drunk, did that mean he was bewitched? "I think you've cast some kind of a spell on me." Matt spoke his thoughts aloud as he gazed into Kayla's limpid hazel eyes.

Turning slightly, she laid her hands on his chest, feeling the muscular strength of him. She was achingly aware of his virile pulsing, a vital force that made a syrupy warmth flow through her veins like hot honey.

"I was thinking the same thing about you," she said softly. "I've never felt this way before. Not about anybody. And I—I'm not usually this frank, either," she felt obliged to confess. "Disclosure is normally such a risk but with you I feel I can say anything, whatever I'm thinking, and not worry about all those male-female games of strategy." With Matt Minteer, love wasn't a risky chance, it was a sure thing.

Matt groaned. Her sweet confession marked the end of his self-restraint. It was just too much to fight his own instincts, his own needs. The iron self-control that had been both his blessing and his curse, dissolved. He wanted this woman more than he could ever remember wanting anyone, even Debra. He wanted to kiss her, to touch her, to brand her as his. The presence of hundreds of people was, amazingly, no deterrent at all.

Matt lowered his head to hers. Kayla watched him, her eyes smoldering with a hunger she didn't think to hide. He was going to kiss her and she wanted him to, desperately. What did it matter that they were at the head table in the hotel ballroom with the party's political elite, a gaggle of lobbyists and members of the media as eyewitnesses? She and Matt were in love, and as that old song went "Everybody Loves a Lover." In fact, somebody had tried to sing a rendition of that very song tonight.

"Senator Minteer!" The sharp nasal voice of the waiter pierced the intensely private moment, leaving both Matt and Kayla oddly disoriented. "Sir, do you dig the planet Earth?"

Already badly jarred by the untimely interruption, Matt could only gape and mutter, "Huh?" Kayla was too dazed to say a word.

"There is a way to supply energy naturally, without polluting our mother planet...." the waiter continued. His voice seemed to be fading in and out. But he was definitely talking about—

"*Windmills?*" Kayla repeated incredulously. The room was starting to spin again. Or maybe she was the one who was spinning, whirling by lights and tables filled with loud, laughing people. "I—I'm starting to feel as if I'm on a windmill, going around and around." She stared at Matt in confusion.

"It's all right, sweetheart," he soothed, standing up and taking her hand. "It's getting too hot in here. There are too many people and not enough air. Let's get out of here."

She and Matt left the ballroom hand in hand and were approached by a uniformed bellboy as they headed toward the lobby. "Follow me, please," he said.

Kayla and Matt exchanged conspiratorial grins, pleased that this perceptive young man was aiding their escape. They followed him along a quiet carpeted corridor, pausing to steal quick, hungry kisses along the way. The bellboy waited patiently, motioning them onward with a polite, "This way, please."

They trailed after him, stopping when he did, in front of a door. "Here's the room," the bellboy said and opened the door.

"Oh, the room," Kayla repeated, stepping inside. It was very dark. She heard a quiet, "Good night," and then the door closed behind her, blocking out the light from the hall. Now it was pitch-black.

"I can't see a thing," Kayla said. "I have my hand right in front of my face and I can't even see it." She heard someone giggle and realized with astonishment, that it was herself. She was as confused by the sound as she was by the total darkness. Heavens, she never giggled!

"Where are we?" she asked, taking a step into the black void. She stumbled a little. "I could use a Seeing Eye dog," she murmured. "Could we turn on a light?"

"No." It was Matt's voice, deep and husky and whiskey-smooth. Kayla sensed his presence behind her. "If this is a dream, it's the best one I've ever had in my life and I don't want to wake up. Come here, sweetheart."

He reached for her, found her a few steps ahead of him and cupped his hands around her shoulders. The feel of her, her softness and her scent, went to his head like hundred-proof whiskey. His mind was reeling; his body, already taut with arousal, hardened to a level of pleasure so intense it bordered on pain.

He wasn't sure if he'd turned her around or if she had done so herself. Now, however, she was facing him, her body touching his, the warm thrust of her breasts against his chest, her thighs brushing his. He couldn't see her, but he could touch her and smell her perfume, a sultry scent that stirred him deeply. He could hear the soft quick breaths she took and knew that she was as aroused as he was.

"You're my dream girl," he whispered. His lips brushed the top of her head. Her hair was silky and smooth and smelled and felt wonderful. "I mean, my dream woman," Matt corrected himself, chuckling softly.

"Very good, you remembered," Kayla said with a light little laugh of her own. It was natural and easy and right for her to nestle closer to him. She felt so emotionally attuned to him, that being physically close to him was a necessary and natural extension of this mystical meeting of their minds.

"But I'm not a dream," she added softly. "I'm as real as you are." As real as the trembling in her limbs and the searing, liquid heat deep in the most secret part of her. Needs and emotions that she'd long kept locked up inside her came burgeoning to life.

As if of their own volition, her arms twined around his neck, pressing her even closer to him. It seemed impossible to remain still in his embrace and she squirmed and wriggled sensuously against him. Matt moaned and gripped her bottom, lifting her higher and harder against him.

She was clinging to him, her head spinning, as he whispered incoherent words of love, sexy words of passion, into her ear. The dark seductive intimacy was intensely potent, yet that same odd aura of unreality that she'd experienced earlier once again enveloped her.

"Maybe this a dream," Kayla mused bewilderedly. "But how can we both be having the same dream? Or are we? Am I dreaming this or are you?" The concept seemed imponderable. "You must be in my dream because if I were in yours, I—"

"I just know that I want you desperately," Matt interrupted, his voice soft and low and urgent against her ear. He was beyond esoteric discussions. Both thinking and talking required powers of concentration that he did not possess at the moment. His body had taken over; he was aching for her, his forceful need obliterating all else. "I don't care if you're real or a dream," he breathed. "Let me have you, sweetheart."

Kayla felt his lips close around the sensitive lobe of her ear, felt the exquisitely light bite of his teeth. His body was hard against her, his rousing male need unmistakable. She clasped him to her, arching into him.

"Yes, darling," she heard herself say in a hungry, sexy voice she had never heard herself use. She'd never called a man darling before, either, but it came naturally tonight. Matt was her darling, the man she had been waiting for all these years. She'd known it from the moment she had gazed into those gorgeous blue eyes of his, and everything that was happening between them now confirmed her initial instincts.

Matt's mouth took hers in a deep, wild kiss that grew progressively deeper and wilder. His tongue penetrated the sweet moist cavern of her mouth, probing and stroking and claiming it in a possessive display of pure male mastery. Kayla responded ardently, making claims of her own, as passion built and grew within her.

Unable to stop himself, Matt slipped his hand inside her jacket and covered her breast with his palm. Even through the silky layers of her blouse and lingerie, he could feel the tight, aroused nipple. His fingers traced the shape of it and sensuously, lightly tweaked it.

Kayla felt a spasm of fire sear her. A breathy little moan escaped from her throat. Her hands trembling, she pulled off her suit jacket, then reached blindly for his. It was so dark in the room, the blackness lending a surrealistic element to what seemed to be a combination of a fantasy and a dreamy fulfillment of a long-anticipated destiny.

They tugged and pulled at their own clothes, at each other's, discarding garments at a furious clip, pausing for hotly intimate kisses and caresses that grew bolder and more demanding with every stroke.

And then they were lying down. Somehow, despite the lack of light and their unfamiliarity with the room, they had moved instinctively to the bed. Kayla was vaguely aware that she was naked, that Matt was naked, too. The rough material of the bedspread felt sensuously abrasive against her bare skin, another stimulant to her already overloaded senses.

"I want to look at you, I want to see you," Matt breathed with a harsh moan, but he couldn't for the life of him roll away from her to find the light that surely must be here somewhere. "Next time," he promised, his mouth opening over her parted lips once again.

Next time. Yes, there would be many, many of those, Kayla thought dizzily. She didn't know if her eyes were open or closed it was so dark, but it didn't matter anyway. She was far too absorbed in feeling his satisfying masculine weight upon her, crushing her deliciously into the mattress, making her feel small and soft and feminine.

His big hands unerringly found her breasts, warm and full and exquisitely soft. He fondled them and massaged them tenderly, tactilely learning their size and shape. "Tell me what you like," he murmured.

He wanted to pleasure her; he loved hearing her moan and sigh as he touched her with his lips, with his fingers. She was so responsive, so excitingly uninhibited, and he reveled in her open sexual honesty as much as she savored his own unreserved responses to her.

"It feels so good." Kayla sighed softly. "Everything you do to me, Matt. When you kiss me, when you touch me."

She shivered as streaks of sexual tension, of arousal and excitement, rocketed through her.

They kissed again and again, searing intimate kisses that previewed and simulated what was to come, her intensity matching his, their desire surging wildly.

The wiry mat of hair on his chest tickled her breasts, making them so ultrasensitive Kayla cried aloud when his mouth closed, hot and wet, over one beaded nipple. Clutching his head with her hands, she rolled her head back and forth against the mattress, chanting his name.

Matt suckled her with his lips while his hands glided over the supple sleekness of her skin. He was excruciatingly aware of every sensual detail about her—the breathy little cries she made, the feel of her soft abdomen against his own hair-roughened skin, the touch of her small hands trailing over him, petting him, loving him.

Kayla felt a ferocious need burning in her as her body opened to his enticing male heat, like the moist petals of a flower unfurling in the sun. Her whole body quivered as his hand stroked her thighs, up and down, back and forth, until finally moving to the vulnerable softness between. Kayla gasped as he touched her intimately, caressing her with his fingers that were provocative and bold yet so very gentle and knowing.

She felt the hard, hot thrust of his manhood against her and was achingly aware of a deep empty void inside her, an ache that she knew only he—full and pulsing and male—could truly fill. "Now, Matt!" she pleaded. "Love me now."

"Yes baby," he gasped, his voice slurred with passion. He surged into her as she lifted her hips to accept him, eager and ready for him.

Panting, her moans echoing his, Kayla wrapped herself around him, drawing him in deeper and deeper and holding him tightly to her, inside and out.

The combination of her impassioned response and exciting feminine aggression drove him wild. Matt couldn't hold back a moment longer. He began thrusting into her in a frenzied sensual rhythm that she met and matched. It was fast and hard and hot, and the pleasure was mind-shattering.

And then, suddenly, the heat and the tension peaked to flash point and erupted, convulsing Kayla as her senses exploded in rapturous white-hot waves that shook her with pleasure.

Matt felt her climax beneath him and exultantly found his own release, emptying his virile strength into her.

And it happened again and again during the long, dark magical night. They came together, in a frenzy of excitement or in a drowsy, sweet surge of tenderness. Satiated to the point of exhaustion, they slept for intervals, then awakened with a hunger and need that demanded fulfillment.

They couldn't get enough of each other, they couldn't give enough of themselves. All night long there was just the two of them in their own private universe, merging again and again, separating and then fusing in a never-ending spiral of desire and satisfaction.

Kayla opened her eyes a crack. She was aware of a fierce pounding in her head, as if some merciless fiend were inside it, relentlessly striking her skull with a sharp-edged mallet. And the light...it was blindingly bright. Gingerly she closed her eyes again, aware that even her eyelids were aching. Her mouth was dry, her tongue felt swollen. When she tried to move, muscles she'd previously been unaware of seemed to come screaming to life, making her moan with discomfort.

Matt turned his head on the pillow toward the sound of the muffled cry. He'd awakened moments ago to the worst headache of his life and his mouth felt as if he'd slept with a wad of wool stuffed inside it. When he swallowed, a sickening wave of nausea tore through him. The symptoms alarmed him. Had he contracted a swift, virulent case of the flu?

The small noise sounded again and through slitted eyes he saw a mane of long, light brown curls spread over the pillow beside him. The woman's face was very pretty but very pale. Wasn't she feeling well, either? He considered the possibility of food poisoning and tried to remember if last night's chicken had tasted odd, then realized he could barely remember eating dinner at all.

But he most definitely remembered making love with a beautiful, sexy woman. Matt tried to take a deep, calming breath. So it hadn't been a dream, it had been real. Just as the beautiful, sexy woman lying next to him was real and not a fantasy produced by an overheated imagination, inspired by a sexually deprived body. He was not sexually deprived now, not after last night....

Memories tumbled through his head, too vivid and far too intense for him to cope with in his current weakened state. He relegated them to back-burner status in his mind; right now he had other things to deal with. Like what to say to the woman who was lying beside him.

What *did* one say in a situation like this? Matt realized how unprepared he was, how much he was dreading the moment. He cleared his throat, a definite mistake. Just that small internal motion nauseated him.

The sound had a startling effect on the woman. Gasping, she sat up abruptly, clutching the sheet around her. "Oh God!" It was more a desperate prayer than an exclamation. "I thought I'd dreamed it, but it's true."

Matt closed his eyes for a moment. He'd been right to dread this. It was going to turn into an emotional scene, and he was not good at emotional scenes. All the ones he'd endured with Debra had proven that. As feminine hysteria mounted, he became taciturn, withdrawn and remote. He couldn't help it; something about melodrama made him stoic.

But he wasn't with Debra now, Matt reminded himself. Maybe things would be different today. Determinedly, he turned on his side to face his lover from last night. The mattress seemed to pitch and roll like a boat on a stormy sea. At least it felt that way to his queasy stomach.

"I just want you to know that I don't do this sort of thing all the time," he gritted out. Each word reverberated inside his head like a gunshot. "In fact, I've never done it before. I mean, I've never gone straight to bed with a woman I've just met."

"Oh!" Kayla was aghast. "What are you implying? That I'm some sort of cheap pickup who does this all the time? Are you accusing me of instigating this? Of seducing you against your better judgment? Are you saying that this is all my fault?"

"No, no!" Matt sat up. "I didn't mean that at all." A fine sheen of perspiration covered his face. He couldn't remember ever feeling worse, either physically or mentally. "Karen, uh, Kristin—" He paused to gulp. What a horribly inopportune time for his vaunted memory for names to fail him!

"Just call me Kayla," she said grimly. This was truly the worst moment of her life, Kayla decided, feeling a hot blush sweep her from head to toe. Waking up naked in bed with a stranger who didn't even know her name.

"You don't have to be sarcastic," Matt snapped, his own temper rising. "It was just a slip of the tongue. I know perfectly well your name is Kristina."

Kristina! Kayla almost screamed. Of course, he thought she was Kristina, that had been yesterday's charade. This nightmare just refused to end. Not only had she hopped into bed with a stranger, she had done so impersonating her sister. In every state capital, in the nation's capital too, there was always gossip circulating about lobbyists who extended their efforts into the bedroom—now Senator Minteer would classify *Kristina* among them!

Kayla stole a quick covert glance at Matt. His jaw, so smooth-shaven last night, was covered with a dark, sexy stubble. He looked all male, earthy and sensual, and Kayla was appalled that whatever spell she'd been under last night continued to possess her this morning. She still wanted him! If he was to extend his hand even halfway, she would grasp it . . .

He did not extend his hand. He bolted out of bed and headed for the bathroom, seemingly unconcerned that he was nude. Kayla knew she should avert her eyes, but they stayed riveted to his splendid male form until he disappeared into the bathroom. Last night it had been too dark for her to see him, but the morning's light revealed that he was as virile and well-built as her hands had discerned in the darkness.

Kayla trembled. He'd displayed no similar interest in seeing her, not even a whit of curiosity. He hadn't even glanced at her, he'd just stalked into the bathroom. She could hear water gushing from the taps.

The insensitive barbarian! The Neanderthal clod! Tears of humiliation swam in her eyes. He was making it obvious that he considered her to be nothing more than an easy pickup, a one-night stand that he was already eager to be rid of. Turning her head, Kayla spied the piles of clothing that littered a path to the bed. There was her oyster-colored jacket, the matching skirt and her rose-pink silk blouse strewn along with his shirt and suit. She saw her shoes and his, lingerie and underwear, mixed together where they'd been discarded in last night's sensuous frenzy.

Kayla went hot and then cold. What had happened to her last night? Even as she sat here naked, her body bearing the physical evidence of last night's passionate consummation, she was still having trouble believing it was true. She'd lost her head over Matt Minteer, thrown away a lifetime of scruples to go to bed with him, a man she'd known only a few hours. They'd spent the night making love with a rapturous intensity she'd never before experienced, never dreamed herself capable of. She hadn't considered herself the type to evoke such urgency in a man. But she had, last night with Matt.

Matt had said that he'd never done this sort of thing before... Well, neither had she! Last night had been totally out of character. She was normally so cautious, so careful and controlled. She never took foolish chances—at least she hadn't until her path had crossed Matt Minteer's.

And now she was left alone to face the consequences of her actions. Choking back a sob, Kayla sprang from the bed and quickly gathered up her clothes from the floor. She haphazardly pulled them on, her ears attuned to the loud rushing of water in the bathroom. Though she badly wanted a shower, it was a luxury she would have to postpone until she arrived back at Kristina's apartment. She had to get out of here before Matt emerged from the bathroom! She simply couldn't face the cold rejection she knew she would see in his eyes.

The water was still running when she slipped from the room. Kayla bypassed the elevators and ran into the stairwell, racing down the steps two at a time. Last night's fantasy of exciting, everlasting love had turned into a chilling phantasm. In the grim light of day Kayla forced herself to face the painful fact—last night's idyll hadn't been about love at all, just lust. What was it that Penny, her stepmother, had often said? Something about love not being a risk, but a genuine hazard? Once again, it seemed that Penny's sense of doomed pessimism had been proven right.

Kayla felt as though her heart were breaking.

Back in the room, Matt emerged from the bathroom, aware that his skin was a ghastly shade of green, that he was cold and clammy and felt sicker than he'd ever felt in his life.

He had turned on the taps in both the shower and the sink to drown out the ignominious sounds of himself wretching. Bad enough that he'd insulted poor Kristina, though he certainly hadn't intended to. For her to know that he'd been dreadfully, helplessly sick would be the ultimate humiliation.

He was definitely not a cool, smooth operator with a lifestyle to match, Matt acknowledged with a moan. Undoubtedly, there were guys who woke up in bed with a woman of only a few hours' acquaintance, men who suavely called room service to order breakfast for two, but Matthew Minteer knew he could not be numbered among them. Breakfast! Even the thought of it was almost enough to send him back into the bathroom.

No, he was not cut out to be one of those cool bachelors. He wanted to be married, to a nice loving woman who would share his life and his career, who would raise a family with him.

Was that too much to ask? he sometimes wondered. His mother had been that and done that for his dad. But Debra Wheeler had rebelled and the few other relationships he'd had, hadn't worked out, either.

Which brought him to today, and waking up with Kristina McClure in his bed after an astounding night of the most spectacular sex he'd ever had. No, he amended. What he and Kristina had shared had been more than sex. The intensity, the depth of their responses, the total and perfect culmination of their desires. It had to have been much more than a casual, recreational romp.

"Kristina," he called her name softly, determined to talk things over, to overcome the awkwardness that had soured their awakening. He turned to the bed.

And saw it was empty. Kristina was not in the bed! A swift glance around confirmed that she was nowhere in the room. Nor were her clothes. Only his littered the floor.

It was all too obvious. She had dressed and sneaked out while he was being sick in the bathroom! Matt sank down on the bed, fighting a volatile mixture of rage and gloom. She was gone. Could she have possibly made it any plainer that she considered their interlude last night exactly that, an interlude? A very temporary one. A one-night stand that was over. She hadn't even waited to say goodbye. She'd just left.

Just when he thought that it couldn't get any worse, that he couldn't feel any worse, a knock sounded at the door, a sound so loud that he covered his throbbing ears to mute the thundering echoes in his head.

"Matt, open up, I know you're in there!" his brother Luke's authoritative voice called through the door.

Matt scowled. What an abominably unlucky day this was turning out to be. Kristina had fled and now he'd been tracked down by his younger brother, the quintessential cool bachelor himself, who knew all the right moves and all the right words. Had Luke Minteer awakened to find himself in bed with a naked sensuous beauty, Matt was sure there undoubtedly would have been an entirely different outcome than the hapless scene that had just been enacted.

He groaned. No, it really couldn't get any worse than this.

Three

___

Still feeling nauseated, Matt picked up his clothes and put on most of them before opening the door to his brother. Luke Minteer rushed inside. At thirty, he had the Minteer coloring, dark hair and blue eyes, but his height came from his mother's side, the Hylands. He was five foot ten, the shortest of the four Minteer brothers, a fact he accepted with good humor most of the time.

Six years ago, when he'd first won the state senate seat, Matt had made Luke his chief administrative aide. He planned to do the same when he went to Congress in D.C.

"Are you okay?" Luke frowned with concern as he studied his older brother.

"No." Matt made his way back to the bed and sat down on the edge. "I'm not."

Luke crossed the room to sit down beside him. "Matt, I'm sorry I wasn't there last night. Maybe if I had been, I could have done something to stop it. Damn, I feel terrible about this!"

Matt went rigid. Obviously his brother had found out that he'd gone to bed with Kristina McClure. He sighed. The last thing he needed was a lecture from his little brother. Because even though Luke, who had a law degree, had proven himself an invaluable counsel, he was still four years younger—which made him a kid brother in certain situations. Such as this one.

"Look, save the lecture, Luke. I know it was out of character for me, but we're both consenting adults and—"

"Consenting? Huh? What are you talking about?" Luke interrupted, staring at him.

"About Kristina and me, of course," Matt growled.

"Kristina?" Luke's eyes widened as comprehension dawned. "You brought a woman up here?" He looked around the room. "Where is she? Who is she?"

"She's not here now," Matt declared, stating the obvious. "Her name was—is—Kristina McClure." He imparted the information, reluctant but resigned. Luke was like himself when it came to ferreting out facts. Neither would quit badgering until they got them all. "She's a lobbyist for PITA," he added.

Luke's reaction was predictably on target. "You went to bed with a lobbyist?" He jumped up and began to pace the room, squawking his disapproval.

"Luke, sit down," Matt demanded. "All that motion is making my headache worse."

"The entire party leadership has a headache this morning," Luke said grimly. "Matt, brace yourself. I have a helluva story to tell you. Have you ever heard of a group called WINDS? It's an acronym for Windmills for Near and Distant States."

"WINDS." Matt frowned thoughtfully. "Aren't they that bunch of lunatics who are committed to the idea that windmills will fulfill the country's energy needs? They want to begin their project in western Pennsylvania and have targeted the Johnstown area to build the first windmill farms."

Matt smiled for the first time that morning. "They came to my office a few months ago, I reviewed their proposition and politely sent them on their way. Their idea was a real howler! Windmill farms in western Pennsylvania! The terrain is all wrong, it's mountainous, all steep hills and valleys, and what wind there is is pretty well blocked by the trees—tens of thousands of them! But WINDS didn't burden themselves with facts and statistics. They'd already decided that since windmills work in places like the Netherlands and parts of the Southwest, they can work anywhere, damn the terrain and the trees and anything else. The whole idea was sheer insanity."

"You can say that again," agreed Luke. "Nobody in Harrisburg took WINDS seriously. They've been kicked out of everybody's office, from the governor on down." He paused and cleared his throat. "So they decided to take matters into their own hands. Matt, all the waiters working the ballroom last night were WINDS members. The manager hired them, knowing nothing of their—er—affiliation. They presented themselves as nothing more than extra banquet waiters."

Matt felt an ominous foreboding. "But they weren't really waiters?"

Luke shook his head. "They were the WINDS crackpots who decided that the fund-raiser—featuring you, a native son of their target area—was their big chance to get their ideas across to the party leadership. By hook or by crook."

"What exactly did they do?" Matt asked hoarsely.

Luke shook his head disgustedly. "As waiters and bartenders those crazies had access to all the food and drink in the ballroom. They took advantage of that access to spike everything with a hundred-and-twelve-proof vodka. I mean everything, Matt, even the water. Apparently they thought that legislators under the, uh, influence would be more amenable to their windmill scheme. Hey, you'd have to be either drunk or crazy, maybe both, to take them seriously."

"Drunk!" Matt gasped. "I was drunk?" Oh, he should have known! He recognized all the signs and symptoms now. But how could he have suspected he was drunk when he'd drunk so little? Or so he'd thought. He swallowed hard. "Then Kristina was drunk, too?"

"Everybody was," Luke intoned gloomily. "The only thing to be thankful for is that one of those WINDS creeps saw how blitzed everybody was and panicked at the thought of all those people getting into cars and driving home. He confessed to the hotel night manager who immediately ordered that all the guests be given rooms for the night here at the hotel, free of charge, of course. Luckily this place is enormous. Nobody from the fund-raiser was permitted to leave the premises and everybody was personally escorted to the rooms to, well, sleep it off."

Thinking hard, Matt vaguely remembered following a young bellhop through the corridors last night—to *this* room! He marveled now that neither he nor Kristina had bothered to question the escort or the room. It had all seemed perfectly logical at the time; one didn't question magic in a dream or a fairy tale. And last night had contained elements of both.

"Thank God nobody suffered anything worse than what you're suffering now—a massive hangover," Luke continued. "Damage control is already beginning. The entire incident is hideously embarrassing and everybody there last night just wants to forget it ever happened."

"Forget it?" Matt echoed numbly. He felt his temper flare. "No way! We're going to go after those demented maniacs, we're going to make an example of them that will scare—"

"Matt, believe me, this is no time to be thinking of revenge and retribution," Luke cut in. "Everything about WINDS, from their harebrained windmill scheme to their sabotage of the fund-raiser last night is almost too idiotic to be believed. Nobody—not the politicians or the lobbyists or even the members of the press who were there—want the story to get out because it makes them look like idiots, too.''

"Dammit, Luke, we can't let WINDS off scot-free. What if they try something like this again and—''

"They won't. I've already threatened them with an enormous personal injury suit on behalf of everybody at the fund-raiser," Luke stated, his demeanor as cool as Matt's was heated. "I tossed around threats like bringing in the FBI and FDA, too. If WINDS agrees to quietly leave the state immediately and abandon any plans for future spiking incidents, we won't prosecute. They're already planning to go. They know they've done wrong and are scared to death.''

Matt began to pace the room, agitated, sweating and swearing. "It's not right, Luke. They should have to pay for what they've done.''

"What about this woman, the lobbyist, that you spent last night with?" Luke asked shrewdly. "Do you think she'd like this—uh—incident to become public knowledge? Which is exactly what will happen if you attempt to go after WINDS.''

Matt grimaced. Kristina's flight had made it clear that she didn't care to be linked with him privately, let alone publicly. "I'm certain she wouldn't," he admitted. As much as the injustice of it rankled, he was beginning to see Luke's point. He had to pretend that last night hadn't happened at all and to make that pretense work. To forget it had ever happened. To forget her.

Luke eyed his brother curiously. "So, are you planning to see her again?" he asked.

"See who again?" Matt countered bleakly. "Last night never happened, remember?''

Kayla didn't cry until she was safely inside Kristina's apartment, and then she let all her bottled-up tears flow. She cried for a long time, overwhelmed with confusion, hurt and regret. Finally, exhaustion ended her tears but not the depression or the pain.

She'd somehow deluded herself into believing that she had fallen in love at first sight and then allowed herself to be swept away by sexual passion, believing all the while that Matt Minteer shared her feelings. But he hadn't. His behavior this morning had made his feelings, or the lack of them, quite clear.

Why, why had she done it? Kayla searched for a reason, and an appalling one came to mind. Yesterday's date happened to mark the third wedding anniversary of Scott and Victoria Ceres. The fifth of February, a date Kayla would always remember because it was the very date she had chosen for her own wedding—to Scott Ceres himself. That he had married another woman on that precise date, after abruptly dumping Kayla, was a stunning example of how ruthless and cold-blooded Scott actually was. Everyone had told her she'd had a lucky escape from certain heartbreak.

Kayla, suffering from heartbreak anyway, found the well-meaning words cold comfort. Three years later, she thought she'd finally gotten over Scott, thought she'd put it all behind her, but her behavior last night made her reassess her recovery. Could she have been having some sort of unconscious reaction to the anniversary of their breakup? Was that why she had been driven to find solace with another man?

Except it hadn't seemed at all like solace. It had been hot and wild and sexy and she hadn't thought of Scott at all. She had been totally out of control. Kayla's whole body burned. She had to get out of here! The urge to escape this town and put last night's lamentable lapse of judgment behind her propelled Kayla to action. She threw her clothes into her suitcase, wrote Kristina a brief note and fairly raced to her car.

Unfortunately, she couldn't escape her thoughts as easily as she'd left the city. During the entire drive back to Washington, possible consequences and repercussions haunted her.

What if he'd made her pregnant last night? Kayla's heart clenched. Pregnant by a man who didn't even know her name. Oh, it was too awful to contemplate! So she proceeded to worry about something else instead.

Suppose Matt Minteer regaled the party boys with tales of last night's romp in the hotel bedroom? It would be akin to printing her sister's name and phone number on a men's room wall with the notation: For A Good Time, Call *Kristina*. Kristina McClure would be marked as a lobbyist who slept her way around the state capital!

What could she possibly say to her sister? How could she ever explain?

Later, back in her compact efficiency apartment located in one of the sprawling garden apartment complexes that ringed the city of Washington, Kayla restlessly paced the floor, trying to find the right words and the right way to tell her sister what had happened.

But when Kristina called her on Sunday evening, Kayla used none of her prerehearsed speeches. She never had a chance.

"Kayla, I just wanted to thank you," Kristina said breathlessly, not even bothering with a hello. "Boyd and I spent the whole weekend together and it was the most wonderful time we've ever had. We were able to say all the things that we'd never said before and—" she broke off giggling "—wait, he's trying to wrestle the phone from me. He wants to thank you himself."

"Boyd's there with you now?" asked Kayla.

"I'm here," Boyd himself replied. "I rearranged my schedule to stay over a few more days. I'm flying back to Atlanta on Wednesday."

He and Kayla chatted for a few moments before he thanked her for taking over for Kristina on Friday night so that she could meet him. He added jocularly, "We owe you one, Kayla. A big one."

What could she say to that? Kayla wondered grimly. Kristina and Boyd were obviously deliriously happy, at least for now, so why spoil it for them?

Kristina came back on the line. "We'll have to reschedule our weekend together soon, Kayla," she said happily. "I might not be in Harrisburg too much longer."

"You're thinking of moving to Atlanta to be near Boyd?" guessed Kayla. "I think that could be a good career move, Kristina." Did she dare confess that under the circumstances she'd unwittingly created, it was most certainly an *excellent* career move?

"Of course it isn't," Kristina said dryly. "Career-wise, it's foolish, leaving when I've finally learned all the ropes and made a large number of contacts and have achieved a certain reputation for effectiveness. But this time, I'm putting my personal life ahead of my professional one, Kayla."

Kristina took a deep breath and pressed on, "I know Penny told us to always depend on ourselves and never count on any man, but that attitude is what wrecked everything between Boyd and me the last time. This time I'm going to take a chance on love, Kayla."

Kayla closed her eyes as myriad emotions surged through her. Relief, for if Kristina left Harrisburg she wouldn't have to face the mess Kayla had landed her in. Happiness, because it seemed that Kristina and Boyd were going to work things out after all. And anxiety mixed with apprehension because her sister was taking a dangerous risk, giving up the security of her career for the uncertainty of love.

Because love was most definitely uncertain. Her own brushes with love had ended in either death—her mother when she was seven, her father three years later—or abandonment—her stepmother Penny's two failed marriages after the twins' father's death, Scott Ceres's defection to another woman. And after her recent catastrophe with Matt

Minteer, Kayla was not at all keen on taking emotional risks. They cost too much, they hurt too much.

But she kept her thoughts and her doubts to herself and warmly wished her sister the very best. All too often, Penny had squashed the twins' romantic dreams with a few words of cynicism, always offered with the best of intentions, yet bringing a demoralizing discouragement all the same. Kayla didn't want to put a damper on Kristina's happiness. Perhaps, deep inside her, the dream that true love really did exist, that there really were romantic happy endings, still flickered.

She wanted to believe it was possible and maybe some-day... someday it would happen for her. But it hadn't happened with Scott Ceres and it wasn't going to happen with Matt Minteer. Involuntarily, her thoughts drifted back to that moment in the ballroom when her eyes had met Matt's startling blue ones. Her heart began to beat faster, just as it had at that moment on that night. She felt like crying again, but this time she succeeded in holding back her tears.

Nature willing, she would forget that night had ever happened. And no matter what—why, not even if she ended up pregnant with quintuplets!—would she ever see or speak to Matt Minteer again. She promised herself that.

Matt spent a typical hectic Monday, beginning with a legislative breakfast with one of his corporate constituents, followed by a caucus meeting prior to going into session. By twelve-thirty, he was in his office to talk with Luke, his chief of staff. He went to lunch with some colleagues and then he met with an attorney for the Legislative Reference Bureau. After that meeting, he spoke with several constituents who had dropped by his office to discuss district concerns.

But by late afternoon, his schedule was clear; his meetings and legislative duties were finished for the day. With nothing to distract him, he was forced to confront the thoughts he had been blocking. Forget Friday night had ever happened, Luke had advised, but Matt just couldn't let it go.

He finally faced the situation squarely. It wasn't in his character to make love to a woman and then never see her again. He'd always been too discriminating to indulge in casual one-night stands. No matter how old-fashioned his views might be, he did not have sex with a woman he cared nothing about. The very fact that he'd gone to bed with Kristina McClure, WINDS tactics notwithstanding, meant that he felt something for her. He refused to speculate on how much and how deeply his feelings ran, he just knew he couldn't *not* see her again.

Without having any real idea of what he planned to do or say, Matt arrived at PITA's headquarters and was directed to Kristina McClure's office by the sweetly smiling receptionist. He asked the young woman not to announce him, intimating that he was welcome anytime. Her smile never faltering, the receptionist granted his wish, and Matt strode to the door, opening it quietly.

Inside the office, a couple stood clinging to each other in a hot embrace. The sounds of heavy male breathing and breathy female whimpers permeated the silence, burning Matt's ears. He stood stock-still, his jaw comically agape. But he found nothing funny in his untimely interruption.

Although her long, light brown hair was bound in a tight French braid instead of flowing soft and loose down her back, though her face was almost completely blocked from view by the other man, Matt recognized the young woman in the passionate clinch as none other than his erstwhile lover of Friday night. Kristina McClure.

Desperately not wanting to be seen, he started to back out of the office. But he was a moment too late. Somehow the couple must have sensed his presence—or perhaps they simply needed to come up for air—but whatever the reason, they suddenly broke apart.

And turned toward him.

Matt stifled the urge to curse aloud. He was not as successful in tamping the fierce wave of anger that surged wildly through him. He was a fool to have come here, he raged at himself. Worse yet was this feeling of betrayal that stabbed at him. How could she have given herself to him so completely on Friday, only to turn up in another man's arms the following Monday?

"Oh!" Kristina looked startled at the sight of him.

I'll bet she's surprised, Matt thought nastily. She'd been caught in the act. He wondered if her current paramour was another legislator about to fall victim to this spider-woman's charms. Kristina McClure had some way of lobbying! To think he had worried that she would be upset about negative publicity! Ha! She probably would have relished it as a career booster.

She was blushing now, and Matt marveled at how well she played the demure embarrassed maiden, lowering her eyes, smiling sheepishly over at Matt and then at the man in whose arms she still nestled.

"Senator Minteer?" she said in a soft, surprised voice, as if she wasn't positive it was him. "I'm sorry. Did we have an appointment?"

Matt resisted the urge to deck her. He'd never struck a woman in his life and he wasn't about to let this, this little *tramp* incite him to violence.

"No, we didn't have an appointment, Ms. McClure," he said, his voice cold and dripping sarcasm. "I thought I'd drop by to make sure you made it safely to the office."

She looked baffled. Matt was grudgingly impressed by how very believably she could enact bewilderment, as if she had no idea why Senator Minteer should stop by to see her, as if his veiled reference to Friday night totally eluded her. When it came to acting, this girl would give Julia Roberts a run for her money.

"Was there any reason why she shouldn't have arrived here safely?" the other man asked, gazing speculatively at Matt.

Matt noted the possessive hold the guy had on her, the slight challenge in his voice. His tone, his body language stated, "This is my woman." Boy, are you being suckered, pal, thought Matt, and felt a momentary pang of sympathy for him.

Kristina cleared her throat, then smiled. "Senator Minteer, I'd like to introduce you to Boyd Sawyer. He's a research physician for the Centers for Disease Control in Atlanta. Boyd, this is State Senator Matthew Minteer, who has just announced his intention to run for a congressional seat. We're all confident that he'll win and be in Washington next January."

Matt was dumbfounded. How coolly, how smoothly, how innocently she'd pulled that off! Introducing one lover to another. Were they now supposed to exchange pleasantries? Maybe he should ask Boyd Sawyer about his golf game?

Matt suppressed a snort of indignation. The sooner he got away from this female barracuda, the better.

"I wish you the best of luck in your campaign," Boyd Sawyer said with credible sincerity.

The poor sap obviously had no idea that he'd been cheated on over the weekend. Hostility flared within Matt, and it was all directed at Kristina. "Good luck in your medical research," he said to Sawyer. "Hope you find, uh, whatever you're looking for." No use getting angry at him. Boyd Sawyer was simply an innocent bystander.

Matt strode out the door. But he couldn't resist turning to take one parting swipe at the perfidious Kristina.

"Did you tell Boyd about Friday night and the WINDS debacle?" he asked with an extremely hearty laugh. It sounded forced, even to his own ears. He definitely wasn't as skilled an actor as Kristina. Nevertheless, he persisted in his performance. "What a zany bunch of cutups, hmm? I know we're all supposed to have taken a vow of silence about that night but hey, there's no need for secrecy and subterfuge between two old friends like you and me. Right, Kristina?"

He had the satisfaction of seeing her eyes widen in what was definitely, unmistakably, alarm. He wondered what kind of lie she'd told Sawyer to explain her whereabouts Friday night. Probably made up a tale about a sick grandmother or something equally phony. He felt a fraternal link to Boyd Sawyer and hoped the other man escaped from her treacherous spell as easily as he himself had.

For it dawned on Matt as he walked out into the wintry February sunshine that Kristina McClure's potent allure no longer held him captive. He was free. Maybe it was the shock of seeing her in the other man's arms, maybe it was because of her stellar, deceitful performance. Whatever, he realized that today he hadn't looked into her honey-hazel eyes and felt that thrill he'd felt on Friday. He had looked at her soft mouth and hadn't been seized by the desire to kiss it.

Whatever intangible magic, whatever sexual chemistry had drawn him to her was gone. He had gazed at her and not ached with wanting her. In a bizarre way, it was as if he had been with someone else entirely during the passionate Friday night.

And maybe he had. Matt's lips twisted into a cynical smile. He'd been with a figment of his imagination, of his drunken imagination. He had seen what he'd wanted to see in Kristina McClure; he'd made her his fantasy-come-to-life.

Now, in the cold light of day, Matt faced the truth. His dream girl—dream woman—was just that. A dream. A dream that had ended.

Four

———

"Kayla, there's a call for you from your sister," Jolene Fuller, Kayla's secretary-receptionist and all-around gofer, spoke through the intercom before putting through the call.

Anxiety streaked through Kayla. Kristina rarely called her at the office, and they'd just spoken on Sunday evening. Today was only Wednesday. Had Kristina's romance with Boyd Sawyer hit the rocks so soon? Or had word of Kayla's Friday night indiscretion leaked, leaving Kristina to cope with the barrage of nasty gossip? Kayla's heart lurched as she apprehensively picked up the receiver. Kayla knew she should have talked to Kris about it all, but so far she hadn't had the nerve.

To her surprise, Kristina was cheerful and upbeat, chattering on about Boyd who'd flown back to Atlanta earlier that morning, about her plans to visit him, about the unseasonally warm weather Harrisburg was currently experiencing.

Kayla began to relax. It seemed Kristina had simply called to chat, after all. Things were obviously going well with Boyd and she even hadn't mentioned Friday night. Until...

"You know, I've been talking so much about Boyd and myself that I never got around to asking you about that fund-raiser on Friday," Kristina said. "Thanks again for subbing for me, Kayla. Did you get a chance to meet Matt Minteer?"

Kayla bolted upright and clenched the receiver, her heartbeat pounding in her ears. She strained to discern any nuances in her sister's tone but either there were none or she was too rattled to pick up on any. "I met him," she said carefully.

"He's a great-looking guy, isn't he?" Kristina chirped. Kayla said nothing, nothing at all. She didn't trust herself to speak.

"So how did everything go?" asked Kristina, seemingly unfazed by her sister's lack of response.

"Go?" Kayla echoed. Oh, how to answer that? An image of herself and Matt intertwined on the bed in the darkness, touching, moaning, coming, flashed before her mind's eye with such vivid clarity, she nearly cried.

Mercifully, Kristina started talking again, her voice as chipper as before. "Word around here is that it was just a typical fund-raising dinner. I hope you weren't too bored, Kayla."

Kayla tried to swallow and couldn't. "That's all you heard about it?" she dared to ask.

She clearly remembered sitting on Matt's lap at the head table, in full view of the crowd. And there had been no comment on that? Surely it wasn't commonplace behavior at a campaign fund-raiser? Or was it? Perhaps she should revise her perceptions of party politics on the state level.

"Mmm." Kristina sounded bored, as if she were already tiring of the topic. She immediately launched into another.

"Kayla, I do have an ulterior motive for this call. I'm hoping to tap your consulting and media expertise on behalf of a friend of mine, Elena Teslovic. She's a public health nurse who has done a lot of unpaid lobbying for the poor and elderly. She's decided she can do more as an elected official and is planning to run for a seat in the state house against a totally odious incumbent. Would you be interested in taking her on as a client? Before you decide either way, let me tell you something about her."

It took several minutes for the tension to drain from Kayla. More relaxed, she could fully listen to her twin's capsule summary of the candidate, who seemed bright, talented and scrupulously honest, with a desire to serve in political office rather than using it to serve herself.

"She's a political neophyte but she has great natural instincts and she's determined to make a difference, Kayla," Kristina concluded eagerly. "We need people like Elena in public office. Say you'll come and at least meet her. She could definitely use your expertise. You'll stay at my apartment with me, of course."

Kayla considered it. Traveling was part of a political consultant's job and the living expenses incurred while staying in another city was always a concern. Staying with Kristina would certainly ease the budget while she met and assessed a potential new client. She had every reason to accept and under normal circumstances, Kayla would have, immediately.

This time, however, she hesitated. Being back in Harrisburg meant the risk of running into Matt Minteer. Humiliation and shame roared through her at the memory of the uncharacteristic, passionate abandon she'd indulged in with him. No, seeing Matt Minteer again was more than she could face.

"Kristina, I—"

"Do you know that I was in a traffic jam this morning and it took me twice as long as usual to get to my office?"

Kristina cut in breezily. "Harrisburg is growing by leaps and bounds. It's no longer the small town it used to be. Why sometimes I go for *months* without running into people I know."

Kayla was startled. It was uncanny, as if Kristina was attempting to dispel her sister's anxiety by subtly assuring her that it was safe to come to town, that her path wouldn't inevitably cross Matt Minteer's. But of course that was impossible because Kristina had made it obvious that she had no idea what had transpired between her twin and the virile state senator.

Reassured, Kayla considered the matter practically. "I suppose I could come to Harrisburg and meet your candidate. She does sound promising."

"Great, Kayla!" exclaimed Kristina. "I'll arrange a meeting between the two of you. Just say when. I know Elena will accommodate herself to your schedule."

Kayla checked her calendar. "What about Monday?"

"Perfect. Want to come up on Friday and spend that sisterly weekend we didn't have last week?"

"I'd love to." Kayla found herself smiling. She had always drawn strength and comfort from her twin's presence. Kristina was the one person in her life who'd always been there, who stayed while all the others left. Why, they'd been together even before they were born. Yes, a relaxing weekend with her twin sister was exactly the tonic she needed to restore her spirits and get herself back on track after last week's humiliating, shattering debacle with Matt Minteer.

"Dinner tonight will be my treat, Kayla," Kristina said expansively as she pulled her car into the parking lot adjoining the restaurant early Friday evening. "Rillo's is one of the most popular restaurants in town and for good reason. The food is wonderful and the size of the portions is unbelievable! But you'll definitely have to save room for dessert. They have the most delicious homemade ice cream here!''

Kayla felt alarm bells go off in her head. Wasn't this the place Matt had mentioned when he'd invited her to skip the rubber pudding and go out for dessert? Not that they'd ever arrived. They had ended up in bed instead....

She quickly blocked the renegade thought but it took a while for her nerves to stop jangling. The place was quiet and uncrowded and the food as good as Kristina had promised. The sisters made a leisurely meal of it, even splurging on dessert. Kayla deliberately avoided the heralded ice cream, choosing instead a slice of thick rich carrot cake with cream cheese frosting.

A group of six men, all wearing suits in varying shades of gray, entered the restaurant as Kayla and Kristina were leaving. Matt Minteer, deep in conversation with his brother Luke, followed the others who trailed the hostess to their table. He almost didn't notice the two young women who were passing the group, single file in the narrow aisle. But he raised his head just in time to make direct eye contact with Kayla.

Both froze in position, as if they had been suddenly turned to stone.

Kayla was aghast. She'd been in Harrisburg less than three hours and now she was face-to-face with Matt Minteer, the man she had vowed never to see again. All her senses reacted to the sight of him, so tall and strong and darkly handsome. Sensual memories tumbled through her head, and she was catapulted back to that fateful Friday night, just one week ago....

The way he had smiled at her, his eyes heavy-lidded with passion, the sexy, stirring things he had whispered in her ear as he reached for her in the night. The hot, deep thrust of his body into hers as she opened herself to him, enveloping him in her aching melting softness.

Kayla felt hot all over. She realized that she wasn't breathing and painfully exhaled a shaky breath as she watched Matt's piercing blue eyes move from her to Kristina and then back to her face again.

"What the hell?" he managed to mutter before the full force of his shock and confusion crashed over him, rendering him momentarily speechless. Was he hallucinating? Standing before him were two Kristina McClures! *Two of them!* Were the WINDS crackpots at it again? Had they somehow managed to spike the chocolate bar he'd eaten for lunch with a mind-altering substance?

The long pause and staredown in the middle of the restaurant did not go unnoticed by the rest of Matt's party. Luke, standing just in front of him, glanced from Kristina to Kayla for a long moment before he moved ahead, gently but insistently nudging the other four frankly curious men toward their table.

Luke's departure seemed to prompt Kristina into action. "Hi, Matt," she said with cheerful aplomb. "I believe you've already met my sister, Michaela McClure, better known as Kayla."

Matt's eyes swept over the two women. No, his eyes weren't playing tricks on him, and his mind was blessedly, chemically unaltered. What he was seeing was a set of identical twins. *Identical twins!* And he immediately knew beyond a shadow of a doubt which twin had shared his bed last Friday night.

"Michaela McClure, known as Kayla," he gritted, finding his voice at last. No, he hadn't lost his mind; instead, he was trapped in a real-life version of a soap opera plot. "But she's *also* known as Kristina, isn't she?"

Kristina looked down. "Well, uh, I guess last Friday she was," she said rather sheepishly.

Matt's eyes burned into Kayla's. The intense physical attraction that he had felt last Friday night when they'd first met surged through him all over again. Accompanying that

dizzying rush, almost overriding it, was a ferocious anger.
How could it be? he wondered furiously. When he looked
at Kristina McClure, he saw a pretty, stylish young woman
who excited him not at all. Yet when he gazed at her identical twin—*her identical twin!*—he saw . . . he felt . . .

"You two must have had a good laugh over all of this."
He attempted to flash an amused, sophisticated smile, but
the result came closer to a hostile baring of teeth. "Do you
do it often? And then compare notes afterward?"

Kayla shivered. Clearly, the twinly deception had infuriated him. He looked like a wolf about to execute a lethal
pounce. Excruciatingly unnerved, she suddenly recalled how
he had so cavalierly left her alone in bed after swaggering
into the shower, without a single word of tenderness or
concern—after placing full responsibility for their actions
on her! It was a most bolstering memory.

Her temper flared to flash point. Mr. Minteer wasn't the
only one with the right to be angry. And what about that
crack he'd just made about "doing it often and comparing
notes afterward"? It was an insult to both her and Kristina, an unmistakable attack on their characters. Kayla
knew she couldn't let that pass!

"What do you mean, 'do you do it often?'" Kayla demanded hotly. As if she needed to ask! The question was
strictly rhetorical.

Matt, however, chose to answer it literally. "I think the
statement is self-explanatory." He struggled to retain his
cool. And it was a struggle. After his hapless trip to Kristina McClure's office earlier in the week, he'd considered
himself cured of the temporary insanity that had claimed
him for that one reckless, passionate night. But now, in the
presence of Kayla McClure—how strange it seemed to think
of her by that name—he felt himself in danger of a relapse.

"Do you do it often?" His words echoed over and over
in Kayla's head. What he really meant was, *"Do you pick
up men and spend the night with them often?"* He'd al-

ready subtly accused her of that the morning they'd awakened in bed together, though he'd attempted an awkward disclaimer. She hadn't bought it, not then or now. Her guilt wouldn't let her; her conscience demanded that she be punished, that he view her as a tramp.

Kayla glowered at him, her insides churning with rage. Even worse was this sickening sense of betrayal sweeping through her. Though it was paradoxical, considering her own opinion of her behavior, it hurt terribly, knowing that he considered her nothing more than a cheap pickup, an easy roll in the sack.

Not that she would ever let him know. Defensively, she chose anger over pain. "The statement is self-explanatory," Kayla mocked caustically, imitating his every inflection. "Yes, all your insults are self-explanatory, aren't they? You're the quintessential straight-talking politician who never says what he doesn't mean and always means what he says. Or so you claim."

"Insults?" Matt was nonplussed enough to let *her* insult slide. "What are you talking about?"

"It's self-explanatory," Kayla snapped and attempted to stride past him. Unfortunately, her exit was thwarted by his failure to remove himself from her path. He remained right where he was, solid as a rock, blocking her way.

"Get out of my way!" she heard herself say. Her wrath seemed to be increasing exponentially to every second she spent in his presence. The sound and fury of her anger astonished her. She'd never behaved with outright hostility, no matter how great the provocation. In her profession, image must always prevail; one kept a cool head and stayed polite regardless. And she always had, until now...

"No. You're not going anywhere, *Michaela*. Not until I get an apology for your wild accusations and an explanation for that deceitful little game of yours last Friday." Matt's voice matched hers, note for primitive note.

Kayla gaped at him incredulously. "If anyone deserves an apology and an explanation, it's me, you insensitive, self-involved snake! And if you don't step aside this instant, I'll—"

"Uh, people are starting to stare," Kristina cut in quickly. "Why don't you two finish this somewhere else, preferably in private?" She dug deep into her purse and pulled out a set of keys. "You can use my apartment while I head to the mall. I have an awful lot of shopping to do, so I'll just be on my way while you—"

"Not so fast!" Matt's commanding tone halted Kristina in her tracks. "You're as guilty as your sister, Kristina. Perhaps more so. You broke some major rules by having your twin take your place at the fund-raiser, you know. That was a job-related function and sending your sister in your place was blatant fraud. Does PITA know that their lobbyist sends in a double when she has other things to do? And to add insult to injury, you sent a double who knows nothing about their interests!"

Kristina looked chastened. "I agree with everything you've said, Senator Minteer. I do plan to hand in my resignation." Her eyes brimming with tears, she turned to Kayla. "I feel terrible, Kayla. I really left you holding the bag and I don't blame you for being angry with me. I—I wouldn't blame you if you never wanted to see me again!"

Kayla's temper flared. "Oh, give me a break, Kristina. If I had a dime for every time you said you wouldn't blame me for never wanting to see you again, *my* life-style would be featured on *Lifestyles of the Rich and Famous*. You say it every time you do something that makes me mad."

"But this time I really mean it!" cried Kristina. "Kayla, I really do!"

"You two can sort this out later," said Matt, growing impatient with the interruption. He took the keys Kristina was still dangling and fastened his other hand around Kayla's wrist, "Come with me," he ordered Kayla and took a step toward the entrance.

Kayla didn't budge an inch. "Take your hands off me!" She hated that her voice was a choked whisper and that her pulse was racing; she hated the tight, clutching sensation deep in her abdomen. Above all, she hated Matt Minteer for affecting her this way. "If you think I'm going to Kristina's apartment with you, you're—"

"If you'd rather go to my place instead, that's fine with me," Matt interrupted, his voice firm and commanding and utterly confident. "We have a lot to talk about and it's obvious, we can't talk here."

"We have nothing to talk about. I have absolutely nothing to say to you." The words fairly tumbled from her mouth.

"We'll go to my place, Michaela," Matt said decisively, as if she hadn't spoken at all. He handed the keys back to Kristina.

"I'm not going anywhere with you!" Kayla tried to wrench her wrist free. And failed. Matt's grip was an inexorable as a handcuff.

"Why not? You had no qualms about going to that hotel room with me last week and we know each other a whole lot better now than we did then."

Kayla raised her free hand to strike him. Matt caught it in midair and lowered it to her side. Now he had both her wrists manacled, and he held her fast, gazing down at her with hot, piercing blue eyes.

Shaking inside and out, Kayla stared back at him. The look in his eyes was dark and dangerous. Compelling. And infinitely exciting. She caught her breath.

"What's going on here?" Luke Minteer joined them, his voice low and a little frantic. "For Godsakes, it looks like the two of you are about to slug it out right here in the middle of Rillo's, with the governor's chief of staff and the state secretary of commerce and their aides looking on." He cast a quick glance to the table where the four gray suits were watching avidly from behind their menus.

"Slug it out?" Kristina repeated dryly. "I don't think so. Guess again, Mr. Minteer."

Luke scowled. "Well, whatever is going on, this is neither the time nor the place for it."

"I agree," said Kristina. "That's why I think they should leave and—er—sort things out between them elsewhere."

"Leave?" Somehow Luke managed to convey a howl of protest in a mere whisper. "Matt, you can't leave! You're supposed to be having dinner with those very important people at that table over there to discuss the funding to upgrade that old rolling mill into a new specialty steel plant in Johnstown. Think of what that'll mean to the district, Matt. You just can't waltz out of here, without a thought to the area's economic development, not after all the work we've put into this proposal. You have too many people depending on you!"

His brother's impassioned words hit Matt like a splash of icy-cold water. For the first time since seeing Kayla tonight, he remembered his dinner meeting, why he was here and who he'd come with. Slowly, almost dazedly, he dropped Kayla's hands. He was horrified with himself, with his loss of control, with the entire situation. How could he have forgotten that the governor's chief of staff and the state secretary of commerce and their top aides were sitting at the table, waiting to hear his pitch on why his district should receive a portion of the state's economic development fund?

His gaze swept compulsively over Kayla and he felt that same powerful, enthralling feeling of desire envelop him once again, just as it had last Friday night. He had whimsically thought then that he'd been bewitched by her, not realizing that he had been under the influence of alcohol through WINDS's machinations. But what about now? He wasn't drunk, yet she was affecting him just as potently, and he was behaving just as mindlessly. He was appalled. And wildly, hopelessly intrigued.

For the second time in his life Matt Minteer wanted to cast aside duty, self-control and common sense and let his emotions lead him. But he couldn't, he simply couldn't. He had a tableful of prominent political chieftains waiting to be convinced that his district needed that grant. The competition for such funding was fierce and he knew he had a convincing case to present. His economically depressed district needed that new steel plant and he could get it for them. His own needs and desires *had* to be put on hold. Exerting the steely self-control that had always infuriated his ex-almost-fiancée Debra Wheeler, Matt made his decision.

"We'll talk later," he said tonelessly and turned to follow the quick-stepping Luke back to the table.

"We will not!" Kayla whispered after him. "I never want to speak to you again. I never want to see you again!"

Kristina slipped her arm around her twin's waist. "Let's go, Kayla."

Kayla wriggled free and stalked ahead of her. "This was no accidental meeting. You planned this, didn't you?" she accused as they headed to the parking lot. "You invited me to visit for the weekend and then you suggested we come here, knowing full well that *he* was going to be here! Oh, Kristina, how could you do this to me?"

"I felt I owed it to you," Kristina said glumly. "Kayla, I don't know what happened between you and Matt last weekend—um, that is, I have a fairly good idea what did—but—"

"I don't want to talk about it or about *him* ever again, Kristina!"

Kristina was silent for a full thirty seconds. And then, she said, "Kayla, I've been hearing all sorts of weird rumors and gossip about that fund-raiser and more than one person has cast less than subtle innuendos about my style of lobbying."

The sisters got into the car. Kayla buried her face in her hands and groaned. "Oh Kristina. I'm so sorry! I know I should've told you what happened on Friday night, but I was so mortified and confused that I just didn't know what to say or how to explain. All week I've been worried sick about what people might be saying about you and Matt Minteer. The last thing I ever wanted was to wreck your reputation."

"And the last thing I ever wanted was to get us both into trouble, but I did a spectacular job of it anyway," Kristina said morosely.

Kayla sighed. "We were both in the wrong and the way things have worked out makes us more or less even. There's a bizarre sort of justice in that. Kristina, let's make a promise right now to never, ever switch roles again."

"I promise!" Kristina said fervently. "But Kayla, no matter how wrong we were, something good did come out of it. You did me a tremendous favor by going to that dinner and thanks to you, Boyd and I are back together. I can never, ever repay you for that. But I wanted to try. That's why I thought I'd help you straighten things out with Matt Minteer."

Kayla's head shot up. "Let's get one thing straight, Kristina. I don't want to straighten things out with Matt Minteer. I don't want to have anything to do with him. I—I don't want *him!*"

"It didn't look that way a few minutes ago," Kristina said archly. "In fact, it looked as if you were on the verge of leaving with him. If that pesty brother of his hadn't interfered, I'll bet the two of you would be on your way to Matt's place right now."

Kayla flushed scarlet and shook her head vehemently. "No."

"If only Matt would've said 'to hell with party polls and state funding, I have personal business that comes ahead of everything!' " Kristina lamented.

Kayla gave a scornful laugh. "You know as well as I do that politics supersedes anything and everything in a politician's personal life. Not that it matters to me what Matt Minteer does. I have an aversion to the man, Kristina. I still can't understand whatever possessed me to—" she paused, flushing and breathless "—to *be* with him that night but—"

"You were drunk," Kristina interrupted baldly. "And so was he. So was everybody there. What went on at that fund-raiser is the worst-kept secret in Harrisburg."

As they drove back to her apartment, Kristina explained what she'd heard about WINDS and their beverage-and-food spiking tactics. Kayla was shocked, horrified, humiliated and infuriated—all at the same time.

"I want to press criminal charges. I want to sue!" she raged. "I was drugged, my constitutional rights were violated and—"

"And WINDS is long gone," Kristina said flatly. "From what I've heard, they'd all left the state by Monday morning, and they didn't give a forwarding address. The consensus among the powers-that-be is to simply pretend that the whole mess never occurred. The official party line is that Matt Minteer's fund-raiser went as planned, without a hitch, although I've been getting quite a few sidelong, speculative looks and more than the usual number of propositions."

"Oh, Kristina, it's so unfair. You were with Boyd the whole time and I was the one who—who—" shuddering, Kayla forced herself to say the words "—behaved like a slut."

"I don't believe that and neither does Matt," Kristina said firmly.

"Oh, but he does! He—he—"

"Matt came to my office on Monday afternoon, Kayla," Kristina cut in. "That was the first inkling I had that something, uh, out of the ordinary had occurred at the fund-raiser. Unfortunately, he caught Boyd and I in the middle of a very passionate kiss.''

''And?'' prompted Kayla, curious about his reaction in spite of herself. ''What did he say? What did he do?''

''Keep in mind that he thought I was you. In his eyes, the woman he'd—er—*been* with on Friday was now in a hot clinch with another man on Monday.''

''He acted as if *you* were the town tramp!'' Kayla surmised hotly. ''He didn't bother to conceal his contempt.''

''But before that, before he put up his guard, I saw his face, Kayla. I saw the look in those gorgeous blue eyes of his. He looked...crushed. I knew I had to let him know that you weren't me and that I was someone else entirely.'' Kristina loosed an exasperated sigh. ''Oh, it sounds ridiculous but you know what I mean.''

Kayla grimaced. ''I know you meant well, Kristina. But I just want to put the whole thing behind me. Maybe pretending that nothing happened *is* the best way to handle this, after all. Now tell me, is there really an Elena Teslovic or did you invent her just to get me to Harrisburg this weekend?''

Kristina brightened. ''There really is an Elena Teslovic and you really do have an appointment with her on Monday. Taking her on as a client is going to be well worth your time and effort.''

''I certainly have the time to take on a new client,'' Kayla said wryly. ''My roster isn't exactly growing by leaps and bounds. I believe in substance over style and too many candidates opt for the reverse and go with agencies like Dillon and Ward. It's like Penny always says—''

''Kayla, please don't quote our stepmother to me. An advice maven, she isn't.''

''But she is one, Kristina. For pessimists and cynics. If she ever decides to get out of the real estate business, she could write viewpoint-affirming books for the chronically downbeat.''

"I have the perfect title for her first one," said Kristina, getting into the spirit of the game. "How about *How to Achieve Success and Have a Perfectly Miserable Life in Spite of It?*"

"The book could be divided into four parts," Kayla suggested. "The four *D*'s by which Penny lives—Distrust, Disbelief, Disappointment, Disillusionment."

"We've adopted those four *D*'s and lived by them too, Kayla," Kristina said, suddenly serious. "For far too long. We expect things not to work out for us and we expect people to let us down. It can be a self-fulfilling prophecy."

"We're both successful professionally," Kayla reminded her, but she knew her protest was a weak one. It wasn't professional success that had been a problem for her or Kristina. Or for Penny, either. It was in their personal lives that the four *D*'s reigned supreme.

The twins were silent for a while, each lost in her own thoughts as Kristina steered the car along the highway. And then she turned to Kayla and said brightly, "We're letting Penny's gloom-and-doom philosophy get to us again. It's Friday night and we're together. Let's do something fun. Care to sample some of Harrisburg's nightlife?"

"Is there any?" Kayla asked drolly.

"Spoken with true big-city condescension!" Kristina pretended to be indignant. "I'll prove that there's life after dark in Harrisburg. I'll take you to Bootleggers. It's a club right on the riverfront that has this great reggae band. Are you game?"

Kayla shrugged. A night on the town in Harrisburg was not high on her list of priorities, despite Kristina's attempts to make it sound appealing. She was tired from the long day and left emotionally battered by her encounter with Matt Minteer. The horrifying revelation that she'd been drunk when she'd slept with him had come as a profound shock. She'd never gotten drunk in her life and to do so at this late date and wind up in bed with a stranger...

Perhaps the knowledge should have eased her guilt. After all, she now had the ultimate excuse: *I didn't know what I was doing.* Except that it didn't work for her. No amount of alcohol could induce her into doing something she didn't want to do, she knew that. Consequently, that meant she'd wanted to go to bed with Matt Minteer! And with her inhibitions and defenses conveniently obliterated, she'd done exactly that.

Kayla swallowed hard. She had to stop thinking about that night, to stop thinking about *him!* "Sure, let's go," she said with determined cheer.

Five

Bootleggers, a club on the shores of the Susquehanna River, had wall-sized glass windows that looked out on the dark waters and a dock that enabled boats to pull right up to the club. Inside the wide main room, decorated in hot shades of coral, yellow and turquoise, a six-piece band known as Chill Factor played reggae to the lively crowd.

The Afro-Caribbean rhythm was impossible to resist. While Kristina table-hopped—she seemed to know three-quarters of the people in the place—Kayla sat enjoying the music. It energized her and lifted her spirits. As the drums throbbed and the singer sang a lively calypso tune, Kayla felt herself begin to unwind. She decided she was glad that Kristina had insisted on coming here.

"Luke, I'm beat. All I want to do is to go home and hit the sack." Matt frowned as Luke forged ahead of him, ignoring his older brother's protests, just as he'd been doing since their departure from Rillo's.

"C'mon, Matt. It's time for a little celebration," Luke called over his shoulder. "You just won that grant for the district. Think of the jobs the new steel plant will bring, not to mention the trickle-down effect on the rest of the city's economy."

"It's premature to celebrate," Matt, ever-cautious, reminded him.

"It's in the bag. You sold them tonight," Luke said, grinning with brash confidence. "Now it's time for a little fun. You're going to love Bootleggers. The sax player and the bassist unleash licks that will drive you wild and the percussion sets your blood drumming. I can't believe you've never been here. It's one of the hottest spots to—"

"Meet girls, I suppose," Matt cut in reprovingly. "I've heard all about your adventures, little brother. You have an encyclopedia of pick-up lines and you make every attempt to proceed directly from introductions to bed. Since Steve Saraceni got married and discovered fidelity and fatherhood, *you've* taken over as Harrisburg's fastest zipper."

"I know you meant that as a big brotherly reproach, but I'll take it as a compliment." Luke was cheerfully unabashed. "And it's *women*, Matthew. Women. Girls get testy when you call them girls, unless they're under eighteen or over seventy. And yes, Bootleggers is a good place to meet women, although I really dig the music here too."

Matt was struck by a swift, sharp sense of déjà vu. *"Now everybody in the place knows that you're my girl,"* he had said as he held Kayla on his lap at the fund-raiser last Friday night.

"Woman," she had corrected.

He'd heard her but had been far more interested in the feel of her, warm and soft and feminine on his lap, than in what was politically correct. He remembered what an irresistible temptation she had been, how desperately he'd wanted to slide his hand upward those few crucial inches and cup her breast in his palm, to take her soft ripe mouth in a kiss that was as hard and hungry as his body. Later in the dark privacy of the hotel room he'd done all that and more. . . .

The flashbacks had a visceral effect on him. His body hardened, fast and sharp, and he had to slow his pace and gulp for breath. He blindly followed Luke inside the club and then to a table where the music filled the room, primal and hot and sexy.

The beat of the drums seemed to be throbbing inside him. Matt sank into a chair, ignoring Luke's attempt at conversation. *Kayla McClure.* He turned the name over and over in his mind, hearing it instead of the song lyrics being sung. Her full name was Michaela but she preferred the shortened version of Kayla. He decided he liked both names, that either fit her better than "Kristina."

And it struck him that right now her name was one of the few things he knew about her. While convincing the governor's chief of staff and the state secretary of commerce to invest in his district, he'd successfully banished the Kayla/Kristina conundrum from his mind, but now there was nothing to keep him from reliving the profound shock of seeing the McClure sisters side by side. And knowing, without even being told, which woman had stirred his senses and taken him to heights he'd never believed existed.

And she loathed him. She'd made that perfectly clear tonight by the way she'd looked at him; by the things she'd said. *"I never want to speak to you again. I never want to see you again!"* left little room for interpretation.

"And Dave Wilson wants you to do some campaigning for him in his district," Luke's voice filtered through Matt's troubled reverie. It was a welcome interruption; he hated ruminating and he seemed to be doing a lot of it this past week. Entirely too much of it. He forced himself to concentrate fully on his brother.

"Seems like Dave is starting to sweat out his chances for reelection," Luke continued. "Everybody in the legislature knows what a dirty-dealing, double-crossing arrogant SOB Wilson is, but the voters in his district have been unaware of it...until now. There's this tough-talking nurse who's been stirring up the voters by telling them how and why their man in Harrisburg isn't working for them but against them. People are listening to her and Wilson's running scared. I told him you'd make a few appearances on his behalf and—"

"But I hate the guy, Luke," Matt interrupted, frowning. "Everybody in Harrisburg hates him. He's two-faced, bad-tempered and suspicious. He's managed to stab everybody in the back at least once, from the governor on down. I can't blame the voters for wanting to turn him out of office. He's alienated everyone so thoroughly that he can't get support for any project he proposes. He's actually hurting his district by being in office."

Luke shrugged. "But he's in the party, Matt, and his district borders ours. That makes him a neighbor and a political ally. He endorsed you when you first ran for the state senate and he's backing you for the congressional seat. He could've chosen to fight you for the nomination and run for that seat himself, you know. It encompasses his territory, too. But he stepped aside for you."

"I don't think it was loyalty or altruism that caused him to step aside and leave the field clear for me, Luke. Wilson knows I can beat him."

Luke shrugged. "Motivation doesn't count. Party loyalty is the name of the game, Matt, you know that as well as I do. Anyway, we don't want some renegade nurse who's a complete political neophyte to take—*uh-oh!*"

Matt tensed. "What's wrong?" He turned in his chair to follow Luke's line of vision—and saw a McClure sister sitting six tables away from them.

"I don't know which one she is, but I recommend you stay away from her, from *both* of them," Luke gritted out. "You're obviously not yourself when you're around either one of them and what we don't need is another little scene like the one at Rillo's earlier tonight."

Matt wasn't listening. *He* knew which twin she was and he was already on his feet, heading toward Kayla's table. She didn't see him coming; she was lost in the music, swaying to the rhythm and marveling at the band's ability to dance as they played their instruments.

"Do you mind if I join you?"

Kayla knew who the voice belonged to without turning around to look at the speaker. She'd recognize that husky, deep male tone anywhere. For the past week, it had echoed in her head every night—and much too often during the day as well. Her chest tightened and something hot and wild surged through her. It was rage, Kayla decided. Definitely not excitement and certainly not desire.

"As a matter of fact, I do mind," she said, her frozen tones belying the heat blazing inside her. She kept her head high and straight, refusing to turn and look at him.

"Too bad." Matt pulled out the chair opposite hers and sat down. He was grim and unsmiling, and an unnerving determination glittered in his dark blue eyes.

The table was tiny and the length of Matt's legs caused an unavoidable collision of his limbs with Kayla's. Kayla drew back as if she'd been scalded. She stood up so fast she nearly upset the table. "Since you seemed to have claimed this table, you can have it all to yourself."

She raced off, threading her way through the crowd, toward the neon-lit exit sign. Within moments she was standing outside on a wooden deck that jutted over the rocky shore, overlooking the boats docked beyond. Groaning, she realized that this was not where she and Kristina had come in. To reach the front entrance, she would have to traipse back through the club, where Matt Minteer sat at the table he had commandeered. Where he would be watching and waiting for her?

Her heart jumped, as she headed blindly across the deck, to clutch the thick wooden railing that surrounded it. She had to calm down, she admonished herself. A few more minutes out in the cool night air, a few deep breaths, and she would be in control of herself and up to the daunting challenge of getting out of this place.

Kayla heard the footsteps behind her with a nerve-tingling sense of inevitability. She whirled around to see Matt walking steadily, inexorably toward her. Her breath caught in her throat. She felt perilously rooted to the spot. Fingers trembling, she drew her thick boxy-knit sweater more closely around her.

"Are you cold?" Matt asked, misinterpreting her nervous little gesture. The deck was dimly lit, but he had no difficulty focusing on her figure, which was somehow both concealed and enhanced by the long shrimp-colored sweater that skimmed to her mid-thighs and the tight charcoal gray leggings that clung to her shapely legs.

"No." Her back was pressed against the wooden railing, and her eyes darted frantically, assessing her avenues of escape.

But it was too late for that now. Before she could think, move, or even breathe, Matt was directly in front of her, as close as he could possibly be without their bodies touching. He needed only to lean forward an inch or two to close the gap between them. "Don't even think of trying to run," he said tautly. "You're not going anywhere until we've—"

"You can't threaten me," Kayla snapped with far more bravado than she was feeling. She forced herself to look up at him, to meet his gaze squarely.

Matt stared at her. God, she was a knockout, he reluctantly admitted to himself, even more so than he'd remembered. She was conventionally pretty, true, but she had something else, some intangible charm, some irresistible appeal for him, that evoked feelings in him no one else ever had. It was exhilarating. More than that, it was downright alarming. How could one woman have such power over him?

"And don't think you can scare me with that menacing glare of yours," Kayla piped up. The intensity in his eyes disturbed her, but it didn't scare her. The fact that it didn't—that it drew her, excited her—did. She didn't want anyone to have such a command over her emotions.

"Scare you, threaten you. You have some opinion of me." Matt laughed mirthlessly. "I haven't meant to do either. I just want to talk to you and you make it damn difficult with your penchant for taking off. Is running away your usual style or am I the only one to inspire you to it?"

Kayla was instantly on the defensive. "I wasn't running away from you. I—needed some air and I came outside to get it."

He raised his brows. "And now?"

"Now that I've had some air, I'm going back inside. It has nothing to do with *you*."

"Uh-huh. And what about last week? Saturday morning, to be specific. You disappeared without a word the moment I—"

"Swaggered triumphantly into the bathroom after you'd blithely informed me that the night before was entirely my design," Kayla cut in bitterly. "You couldn't—and wouldn't—be held responsible for anything. Of course I left as quickly as I could. You'd made it obvious that I had fulfilled my function and you were eager to dismiss me."

Matt stared at her, baffled. "Are we talking about the same day? Lady, I was there and the scene you just described isn't the one I lived. For one thing, I didn't do any 'triumphant swaggering' that morning. I—"

"Then what would you call that self-satisfied macho strut to the shower? You left me in that bed without a single word or look or—" Her voice was rising and Kayla quickly cut herself off. "I left immediately, as any self-respecting woman would do. And I don't care to discuss it any further," she added in a low, angry whisper. "Now move out of the way and let me pass."

Matt didn't budge. "That 'self-satisfied macho strut' to the shower you thought you saw? What you were really seeing was a frantic, mad dash to the john where I was sicker than I've ever been in my life, thanks to those WINDS cretins who spiked my entire fund-raiser. I didn't dare take time to stop and chat, or even to take a look at you, or I'd have embarrassed myself all over the room."

Kayla stared at him, momentarily nonplussed. "You were sick?"

"Weren't you?" he countered. "Those maniacs laced everything, including the water, with a hundred-and-twelve-proof vodka. Not only was I acutely ill that morning, I was nauseated for the rest of the weekend."

"I wasn't sick."

"Terrific." Matt scowled. "You have the cast-iron constitution of a vodka-swilling cossack, and I get sicker than a callow college freshman after his first fraternity beer blast."

Kayla almost smiled. She quickly restrained herself. She was not about to fall into swapping morning-after war stories; this was still Matt Minteer she was talking to. Matt *"Do you do it often and compare notes afterward?"* Minteer.

"So that's why you took off without a goodbye," Matt said, preoccupied. "You thought I was an insensitive, thoughtless jerk who didn't have time for you?"

"Something like that," Kayla said fiercely. "I might not have been physically sick, but I was sick with regret. I know you'll find this impossible to believe, but last Friday night was totally out of character for me. My sister and I do not sleep around."

"And why would I find that impossible to believe?"

She was about to give him a hearty shove and stride away, but she couldn't resist throwing his accusation back at him.

His own words should wipe that phony, perplexed expression from his face.

It did. But the expression that replaced it was one of indignation. "I wasn't referring to anything sexual! What I meant was—do you and your sister trade places often? Do you step in for each other and then get together to revel in your trickery? A fair question under the circumstances, you'll have to admit."

"I don't have to admit anything!" This time she tried to stalk off, but Matt grasped her wrist and held fast.

"You have to admit this." He gave one fierce tug, dragging her back to him. He wrapped his arms around her and stared down into her wide, startled eyes. "We were good together. Damn good."

Kayla began to struggle. "We were drunk! It was my first and only drunken one-night stand and all I want to do is to forget it ever happened."

The soft and shapely feel of her body against his, the enticing scent of her perfume, had the same potent effect on him as it had last week. He pulled her even closer, feeling the heat emanating from her into him. Her movements, intended to free herself, inciting him to hold her even tighter as his mind clouded in a haze of dizzying reminiscences.

"It was more than that," he said raspily. "And you can't forget anymore than I can."

He leaned down to nuzzle the curve of her neck, his big hands shaping her more intimately to the hard male planes of his body. He felt as if his senses were exploding. Never had anything felt so necessary, so very right.

Kayla inhaled sharply. His masculine size and strength and heat made her head spin. She felt the hard power of his erection pressing against her, felt his hands moving possessively over her, and her knees went weak. His lips nibbled at her neck as he slid his thigh between hers. Pleasure exploded through her. It would be so easy to close her eyes and give in to what she was feeling. To lose herself in this moment.

Yet even as her body responded to him, her mind resisted. She hadn't given him the right to hold her this way or to keep her out here against her will, Kayla reminded herself. But he'd taken those rights and was bent on taking more. Granted, it appeared that she had misinterpreted him a few times, so perhaps he wasn't the thoughtless, snide opportunist she'd thought he was.

But he was still a politician and no one knew better than she that a politician's primary commitment and interests were in getting reelected, not in a romantic involvement. And Matt had made no secret that he despised political handlers and everything that they did. The secret was that she was one.

Kayla managed to slide her hands to his shoulders and push against him. "Let me go, Matt," she ordered and was embarrassed by the husky breathlessness of her voice. "This just isn't going to work out. It can't. You don't *know*—"

"I know I want you and that you want me just as much," Matt interrupted. "Stop fighting me, Kayla. Stop fighting yourself."

The sound of her name on his lips enthralled her. And distracted her just long enough for him to touch his lips to hers.

"I thought I was going crazy this past week," Matt murmured, his lips brushing hers as he spoke. "I wanted you even though I believed you'd dumped me Saturday morning without so much as a goodbye. I wanted you when I saw your sister and her boyfriend and thought it was you." He smiled against her lips. "And I want you now, of course. You can't have a single doubt about that." He slowly, subtly thrust against her, letting her feel the burgeoning evidence of his desire for her.

"You don't even know who I am," Kayla said, moaning softly. It was deliciously disorienting to talk while their mouths were touching, their lips moving against each other's to form the words. And her mind was swiftly losing the internal war it had launched against her body's demands.

"You're Kayla," he said softly. "That's all I have to know for now."

He took her mouth hungrily, sliding his tongue deeply inside to rub and stroke in excruciating sensual simulation. Kayla's fingers unclenched to clutch at him as the sweeping hot tide of pleasure crashed through her. She arched into him, her breasts swollen and sensitive, the tips almost painfully hard. She remembered how it felt to have him stroke them with his long, deft fingers, to have his warm, wet mouth touching her there, tasting her. . . .

She wanted it again. Overwhelmed by the sensual electricity generated between them, her mind shut down. Who could think practically—who could think at all?—when caught up in this tempestuous maelstrom? Kayla gave up and gave in. All her reasons and resolve against him melted in the lusty fire of their passion.

Why was she fighting, anyway? she wondered foggily. She wanted him so much, she *needed* him.

Matt felt the change within her, from her edgy surrender to the full-blown urgency that matched his own. They kissed and kissed, in a frenzy of ardor. His mouth grew rough, his hands firm and insistent, and she responded with a demanding hunger of her own. He remembered the feel of her body moving under his in bed, taking him into the yielding softness of her feminine heat. He wanted to feel it again, all of it, all of her. Now, tonight.

His pulse pounding, he lifted his mouth from hers, but continued to hold her tightly against him. His eyes and his arms were frankly, boldly possessive. "Let's get out of here," he said, his voice rough and husky with need.

Just the sound of it was wildly arousing. Kayla shivered and clung to him with unsteady fingers.

"We can go to your place or mine, wherever you want." His mouth took hers in another long, greedy kiss. Then, keeping one strong arm firmly around her waist, he started to walk her toward the door of the club.

A stiff breeze gusted from the river, whistling through the trees and whipping around them. Whether from the sudden blast of chilly air or from her being in motion or a combination of both, the sensual clouds that had blotted Kayla's mind began to lift.

"I don't have my own place here," she began. "I—"

"Then I guess it'll have to be my apartment, such as it is." Matt grinned. "It's more of an efficiency apartment, I guess, although my sisters refer to it as a closet equipped with a kitchen and a bath." He dropped a quick kiss on the top of Kayla's head and hugged her to his side. "But it does have a bed, king-size, my one and only decent piece of furniture."

A bed. Kayla was thinking clearly now, for the first time since Matt's lips had touched hers. He was intent on taking her to bed, and she, heaven help her, had been all set to go with him. Suddenly, she was thinking, *very* clearly.

"I'm not going to bed with you, Matt." Kayla stopped in her tracks and pulled away from him. "Nothing has changed since—"

"It's too late to play these games, Kayla," Matt cut in, snaking out his hand to cup the nape of her neck. He heaved a weary, frustrated sigh. "I don't know why you'd even want to. You're as eager to make love again as I am and you'll never convince me otherwise. Not after..." His words trailed off. A tremor of desire mixed with frustration ripped through him. It was an effort to keep his voice steady. "Not after the way you just responded to me."

Kayla rubbed her hands up and down her arms for warmth as the wind continued to buffet them. "I don't play games."

Matt gave a sarcastic hoot of laughter. "That, from a woman who likes to take on her twin sister's identity! And is good enough in the role to fool half the town. I'd say you're a master at games, lady."

"Which goes to show how much you know about me," she retorted hotly. "Or don't know about me, starting with where I live. You were so all-fired eager to get me into bed you didn't even pick up on the fact that I said I don't have a place of my own here in Harrisburg."

"What's the big deal? You live with your sister," Matt concluded testily.

"Wrong! I don't live with Kristina, I'm visiting her. I live in Washington, D.C., not Harrisburg. But you're not interested in any of that, are you? You're not interested in learning anything about me. All you want from me is another quick romp in the sack!"

"Oh, hell!" Matt ran his fingers through his hair, tousling it. "Not the old the-only-thing-a-man-wants-from-a-woman-is-sex accusation."

That had been his ex-almost-fiancée's Debra Wheeler's battle cry, hurled at any man who disagreed with her. Since Matt and she frequently disagreed, particularly at the end of their relationship, he'd heard the accusation often.

Which Kayla immediately picked up on. "Sounds like you've heard that a lot! Well, judging from my own experience with you, I can understand why. You meet a woman and immediately rush her into bed and then wonder why she is insulted when you—"

"That's my brother Luke's style!" Matt cut in.

"So it runs in the family, then?" she said, this time cutting in on him. "How appalling!"

"I was going to add that it's not mine," Matt said tersely. He extended his arms in a gesture of pure exasperation. "Why are you doing this? Why are you deliberately picking a fight with me? For Godsakes, I don't want to quarrel with you, Kayla."

"Yes, we both know what you want to do with me and it isn't to talk." Kayla glared balefully at him. "It's not getting to know me or trying to understand why I might have reservations about jumping into bed with you, either."

Matt groaned. "Here it comes. The standard you-men-are-all-alike, you're-all-insensitive-sex-maniacs-ruled-by-testosterone bit." How many times had Debra used that self-serving feminist decree on him? Too many times, and he'd heard the corollary from her just as often. "Whereas you women, of course, are always driven by pure and selfless human emotion."

Kayla folded her arms in front of her chest in classic defensive mode. "Stop generalizing. It's counter-productive, not to mention annoying. Furthermore, you'll never win a debate or score any real points by trying to divert the issue at hand with—"

"You sound like you're giving a lecture in mass media arts." Matt grimaced.

"It so happens that I'm well-qualified to do so." Kayla drew a deep breath. "Here's another fact you don't know about me, Senator Minteer. I'm one of those consultant gurus, one of those wicked practitioners of political black magic who creates the slick commercials and the buzz-words and the sound bites that have corrupted American politics. According to you, my fellow media wizards and I are personally responsible for everything that's wrong in the modern age. Ah, but why stop there? We pollsters and consultants and media coaches are actually to blame for the decline of all Western civilization!"

Having dropped that bomb, she fled inside, the image of his stunned expression seared into her consciousness. She ran—quite literally—into Luke Minteer as she reentered the noisy, smoky room. The impact of the collision slightly winded them both. They stared at each other for a moment, assessing—Kayla, nervous and edgy, Luke, cool but visibly annoyed.

"Is Matt out there?" Luke asked in clipped tones.

Kayla jerkily nodded her head.

Luke stared at her through narrowed eyes. He didn't like her, Kayla was sure of it. He considered her a threat to his brother's image because of the scene in Rillo's. And because he knew about last week's tryst, as well? Kayla's face burned.

"There are some people here who want to talk to Matt, if you're through," said Luke.

"Oh, we're through, all right." Kayla lifted her chin and forced herself to look Luke Minteer square in the eyes. "And you don't have to worry about your brother. I saved him from himself." She hoped her smile was smugly superior, hoped her tone and her words conveyed sophistication and insouciance as she glided away to find Kristina.

Six

———

Kayla had done her homework before Monday morning's meeting with Elena Teslovic, studying the reports and information that had been forwarded to her by Elena's volunteer staff. She met with Elena and three of her closest supporters in Kristina's apartment promptly at ten o'clock.

"Are you willing to take me on as a client?" Elena asked immediately after introductions had been made all around. She looked to be somewhere in her mid-forties and was tall and dark-haired, and positively exuding energy and enthusiasm. "I can pay for your services but I have to warn you that my campaign coffers aren't too full."

"But what we don't have in dollars, we more than make up for in enthusiasm and loyalty and willingness to work," a young aide interjected earnestly.

"We'll work out some sort of payment schedule if you should decide to hire me," Kayla assured them. "I've studied everything you sent me about the incumbent, David

Wilson.'' She shook her head. ''He's terrible, one of the worst I've come across in my six years in the political field.''

Elena beamed. ''Honey, we're on the same wavelength. You're hired!'' She grasped Kayla's hand in a hearty shake.

''Well, then, let's get down to business.'' Kayla's smile faltered a bit. This was undoubtedly the moment that consultant-bashers like Matt Minteer expected her to pull out her set of voodoo dolls and begin to stick in the pins. Instead, she removed a number of paper-stuffed folders from her briefcase. Not that Matt would approve of that, either. He'd also announced his disdain of marketing studies and principles when applied to the business of getting elected.

And it *was* a business. Determinedly, Kayla pushed the thought of him from her mind. She wasn't wasting another second on a man she hadn't seen or heard from since Friday night, when she'd left him standing on the deck of Bootleggers. Obviously, he considered her too diabolical to pursue, despite his fierce, sexy insistence that they were ''damn good together,'' that he ''couldn't forget'' her.

He had sounded so convincing! Kayla's lips thinned. Wasn't such insistent sincerity, or at least the illusion of it, the hallmark of the successful politician? Matt Minteer could afford to scorn the communications consultants and analysts who made a career out of helping less talented politicians hone their skills. He didn't need them any more than he needed her.

And what was even more infuriating than his blatant rejection was that it stung!

''You've got the fighting spirit, Kayla,'' Elena Teslovic's voice, filled with approval, jolted Kayla from her reverie. ''I can tell by the expression on your face. You look ready to cram the opposition into a shredder.''

''A lapse on my part,'' Kayla said quickly. ''Never wear your emotions on your sleeve. Even when an emotional display is called for, make sure your emotions are always completely under control.'' She inhaled sharply. ''I suppose that sounds as if I'm some sort of manipulative sneak but—"

"Not at all," Elena interrupted heartily. "Who wants a representative with no self-control? Believe me, honey, one thing I've learned in my years as a public health nurse is how to control my temper—and my tears."

Kayla smiled. She liked the other woman's frankness and can-do spirit. Pushing up the sleeves of her loose plum-colored sweater, she got down to business.

"The first thing you have to do is what you've already been doing, but on a much wider and more organized scale. That is, make sure Wilson's constituents know his voting record. Every voter must be made aware that Wilson is feuding with virtually everyone in a leadership position here in Harrisburg, thus destroying any chance he has of effectively representing his district...."

"Hey, Earth to Matt." Luke Minteer waved his hand in front of his older brother's face. "Do you read me?"

Matt drew back and swatted him away. "Bug off, Luke. I'm thinking."

"You were in another world," Luke said bluntly. "No doubt the same one you've been lost in all weekend."

"I was in the same world as you this weekend, little brother," Matt growled. "In Johnstown for Gram and Pap's sixtieth wedding anniversary. We have miles of videotape to prove it. There are more camcorders at our family get-togethers than at the Democratic National Convention."

"You were there in body only, your mind was definitely somewhere else," Luke persisted. "You successfully fooled most of the family, but I could tell you were on automatic pilot and so could Mom and Anne Marie. I fended off their 'What's with Matt?' inquiries by telling them that you were preoccupied with the new bill you're introducing this week, but I know you weren't. You've lost your head over a sexy little political consultant and frankly, I'm—"

"You're way off on that one," Matt interrupted, scowling.

"Am I? Then you wouldn't be interested in hearing about my meeting with Kristina McClure this morning? I artfully arranged to drop by PITA headquarters and just happened to run into her. She is a looker." Luke smiled wolfishly. "Of course, so's her twin sister, the delectable Kayla. Hey, maybe you and I could arrange a double date? You and Kayla, me and Kristina."

"Get real." Matt stood up. "And then get lost." He headed toward the door of his office. "I'm on my way to lunch."

"I know. With Steve Saraceni. The Milk Producers Association has hired him to lobby price supports. For Godsakes, Matt, snap out of this daze you're in or Saraceni will have you signing over your firstborn child to the MPA. He's a shark and if you jump into the tank without all your wits about you, he'll eat you alive."

"Good metaphor, Luke. Original." Matt flashed a sarcastic smile. He paused at the door, his hand on the knob. He couldn't stand it another minute. Feigning indifference, he asked casually, "What did Kristina McClure have to say to you, anyway?"

Luke grinned broadly. "I subtly pumped her about her sister and she doled out the information she wanted me to have, just like the skilled little lobbyist she is. Care to hear any of it?"

Matt's mouth tightened. "Just one thing. Is she—Kayla—is she really a political handler?"

"She sure is. When a candidate signs on with her, he gets the full treatment—communications and media coaching, advice on how to frame issues, project an image, counter the opposition's strategy. She runs her own small agency now, but got her start with Dillon and Ward Consulting Associates.''

"The mother of all no-conscience image-makers." Matt's dark blue eyes flashed. "For the right price, Dillon and Ward could, and would, present a serial killer as St. Francis of Assisi."

"Yeah, well, it seems the McClure twins share your low opinion of Dillon and Ward. According to Kristina, Kayla was too sweet, noble and high-minded to swim with those sharks, if you'll pardon my excessive use of shark metaphors. After a few years, she quit and opened her own consulting agency."

"Translated, it means that having acquired the necessary skills in skulduggery, she decided it would be more lucrative to cash in on it all on her own," Matt concluded grimly.

"She did take several of Dillon and Ward's clients with her," said Luke. "Only the noble, pure-minded ones, of course. According to Kristina, Kayla McClure only uses aboveboard techniques to win and will only take on clients who meet her high personal standard of ethics."

"Yeah, sure." Matt made a derisive exclamation of disbelief. "Isn't that the line all political consulting agencies put out? I mean, they could hardly do otherwise. Who would hire an agency that promised to churn out whatever lies are necessary to win an election? It would be bad for the *image*. And that's what political handlers are all about—image for a price."

"What a cynic!" Chuckling, Luke reached into his pocket and pulled out a small white business card. "Michaela McClure, Communications Consultants Inc.," he read. "Kristina gave it to me. Apparently she carries some of Kayla's cards along with her own. Sisterly of her, huh? Never know when the opportunity will come along to drum up a little business."

He crossed the office to press the card into Matt's hand. "Interested in hiring yourself a media coach, Matt? Kristina says that Kayla does that and does it well. How about a handler? I bet she's mighty talented at...handling!"

Matt glared at him, his temper rising. "You know, when you were just a bratty little kid and you mouthed off once too often, I used to pick you up and swing you around until you were dizzy and then let go and send you flying. You'd smash into something and go bawling off to Mom, but it did have the effect of shutting you up for a while. Mark and I used to call it knocking some sense into you. I'm still bigger than you, kid. I can still send you flying and I will, if you don't shut up."

"Resorting to physical threats, huh?" Luke laughed, completely unintimidated. "You have got it bad, big brother. Why don't you do yourself a favor and go see the girl? She's—"

"The politically correct word is *woman,* Luke," Matt said grandly. "Now if you'll excuse me, I have a lunch date with a Great White Shark who masquerades as a lobbyist-for-hire."

"Are you sure you don't want to come to dinner with me?" Kristina asked Kayla for the fourth time that evening. "This isn't a working dinner, I'm just getting together with a few friends and we'd love to have you join us."

"It's sweet of you to ask, but I can't," Kayla replied, for the fourth time. "I've got to get back to D.C. tonight. I have a full day of meetings tomorrow, starting with Senator DeCaprio at nine."

"I was hoping you could stay longer. I like having you here, Kayla. It gets lonely, living alone. I'm always very busy, but still..." Her voice trailed off and she shrugged.

"I know." Kayla gave her a swift, hard hug. "You won't be living alone for much longer, Kristina. Soon you'll be with Boyd."

"But I'll be in Atlanta," Kristina intoned gloomily. "Do you realize how far that is from D.C., Kayla? It was hard enough getting used to us living in separate cities, but at least Washington and Harrisburg are less than two hours apart.''

"Atlanta is only a short flight from D.C.," Kayla reassured her. "And we'll call each other all the time. Our phone bills will be higher, but right now you work for the independent phone companies, remember? Maybe you can get a lifetime professional discount.''

She smiled, trying to cheer her sister. Kristina had always had difficulty with separations from her twin; it was Kayla's role to be the strong one and put a positive spin on it. "Anyway, I'll be back here from Sunday through Tuesday to meet with Elena Teslovic and her people. You're going to get sick of seeing me!''

"Never." Kristina shook her head. "Why don't you come on Friday and spend the weekend? I promise not to arrange to run into Matt Minteer this time.''

"It wouldn't matter if you did. Matt Minteer would tuck tail and run at the sight of me. I'm the embodiment of evil to him.''

Kristina scowled. "Then he's a jerk. And so is his brother Luke. During that so-called accidental meeting yesterday, that I know he deliberately engineered, he kept coming on to me, even though I'd made it clear that I was seriously involved with someone else. Luke Minteer thinks he's God's gift to women. At least Matt isn't like *that!*''

"No, Matt Minteer is on a different ego trip. He's the Last Honest Politician.''

Kristina rolled her eyes heavenward. "Remember our pledge, Kayla. Work with politicians, work *for* them, even fraternize with them when necessary, but don't fall in love with one.''

"Don't worry, I won't.''

"Well, I do worry. I remember how that snake Scott Ceres broke your heart and he's a politician.''

Kayla grimaced. "One of Dillon and Ward's biggest success stories. Put your mind at ease, Kristina. I learned my lesson well on that one."

"You're attracted to Matt Minteer," Kristina persisted. "I know it, Kayla. I can tell."

"Your infallible instincts have failed you on that one. I like Matt Minteer just about as much as he likes me, which is to say not at all."

"I didn't say you liked him, I said you were attracted to him, physically. Those are two entirely different things, Kayla."

"Now *you* sound like Penny. And I can do without a Penny-on-men lecture. Lord knows we heard enough of them growing up. No wonder we're so mixed-up when it comes to men."

"I'm not mixed-up anymore," Kristina said, her hazel eyes glowing. "I'm sure of Boyd and his love for me. Someday it'll happen for you too, Kayla, you'll see."

"Is that my cue to sing a few bars of 'Someday My Prince Will Come'?" Kayla gave her sister a gentle shove. "Get going or you'll be late. I'll grab a sandwich here and then be on my way." The sisters hugged.

"See you on Friday!" they both called as Kristina left the apartment.

Kayla had taken one bite of her grilled cheese sandwich when the doorbell rang. She frowned, debating whether or not to ignore it and finish her sandwich while it was warm, or answer the door and let it cool and congeal and become inedible. If she were at home, she would've definitely opted to eat and ignore, but since this was Kristina's apartment, Kayla trudged dutifully to the door. She didn't have the right to ignore her sister's caller. It might be an important document being delivered or an invaluable tip from a colleague or—

Matt Minteer? Kayla stared through the peephole. Her heart began to thud. She couldn't remember being this flustered since way back in the seventh grade when Danny

Bryan, the class heartthrob, had sent her a valentine. The sudden sharp memory snapped her back into focus. Get a grip! she admonished herself. Dan Bryan had sent valentines to at least ten other girls in the class that year, too. And she was certainly well past the vulnerable age of twelve.

"Kayla, I know you're in there," Matt called. "I talked to Kristina in the parking lot and she told me you were here." He rapped again. "I want to talk to you and I'm not leaving until you open the door."

Kayla tried to calm herself. There was no reason to panic; if there was one thing she knew how to do, it was how to finesse her way out of a tight situation. She'd made a career out of doing it for others, after all.

She slowly opened the door to him. He was wearing his navy pin-striped suit, which she knew from her own research was the civilized male symbol of authority. She herself advised candidates to wear such a suit when an appearance of intimidation was useful in debating the opposition. Kayla sucked in her breath. *She,* however, was not intimidated by his power suit or by the man himself.

"The door's open," Kayla said coolly. "Talk. You have—" she glanced pointedly at her watch "—five minutes."

Matt stared at her. She was wearing a short plaid skirt, black tights with suede ankle boots and a black shirt covered by a long red blazer. Her long curly hair was pulled high into a thick ponytail. "You look more like a college girl than a slick media wizard," he blurted out.

"Slick media wizard," she repeated tautly. "That's it. You just forfeited your five minutes." She started to close the door, but he was too quick for her. He caught it with both hands and pushed, keeping it open.

"We're going to talk," he said firmly.

"Why? I've already heard your opinion on political handlers and *slick media wizards*. So why waste your precious time talking to me?"

Matt frowned. "Look, can I come in? I'm getting tired of standing out here in the hall arguing with you."

"So you want to come *inside* and argue with me? I'd rather not, thank you. I'm in the middle of my dinner."

Matt gave up waiting to be asked inside and simply came in on his own. Unless she wanted to block him physically Kayla had no choice but to stand aside and let him in. She was not about to risk any physical contact whatsoever. Scowling, she returned to Kristina's small kitchen table where her sandwich laid unappetizingly on the plate.

Matt followed her. "That's your dinner?" He made a face. "Ugh. Not much of a cook, are you?"

"I can defrost and heat things in the microwave as well as the next person," Kayla retorted.

"Well, it looks like you nuked that sandwich. Want to get some Chinese takeout? My treat."

Kayla picked up her sandwich. It was hard and cold. She laid it back on the plate. "I can't. I'm leaving for Washington tonight. As soon as possible." She sent him a withering glance. "If you'll excuse me, I have to finish packing."

It was definitely a cue for him to leave. Kayla started out of the kitchen, expecting him to follow her so she could show him the door. Instead, he sat down on one of Kristina's ladderback kitchen chairs.

Kayla whirled around to glare at him. "You have to leave right now, Matthew Minteer."

"First, answer one question for me, Kayla. It's something that's been bothering me and I need an answer."

Kayla sighed. "I'm probably going to regret this, but go ahead and ask."

He leaned forward, his gaze intense. "Why are you in the field you're in, Kayla? Whatever made you to want to work in such a—"

"Some little girls dream of growing up to be ballerinas or nurses or teachers," Kayla cut in. "*I* dreamed of being a political handler. From the time I was in kindergarten, I pictured myself mapping out campaign strategy, crafting newsworthy sound bites for the six o'clock news.''

''Turning American politics into a corrupt big-money game,'' Matt interjected sharply.

''Oh well, there's that, too,'' she said flippantly. ''All part of the dream.''

''You can make jokes, but it's not funny, Kayla.'' Matt stood up, balling his hands into fists. ''Don't you see what's happened? In politics today, it's no longer a matter of what a candidate has to say, but how many millions he can raise from special interest groups and how those millions are spent by the vultures who create slick media pieces. The ordinary voter feels powerless and left out and he is, because of dissemblers like Dillon and Ward and—and—''

''Me,'' Kayla said flatly.

''Yes. You.'' He walked toward her. ''Kayla, I've thought about this. Hell, I've thought of nothing else since Friday when you told me what you do, what you are.'' Matt came to a stop a few inches away from her. He was breathing fast and hard, his pulse pounding. ''I firmly believe that a person *is* what he or she *does,* Kayla.''

''You believe that a person's occupation is directly linked to his character, or the lack of it?'' She gave a derisive laugh. ''How simplistic can you get! What about corrupt cops or nurses who kill their patients? And where do those television preachers who bilk their believers fit into your tidy scheme of things?''

''I don't think occupations define character as much as actions do. And there are exceptions to every rule, of course, but—''

''Then you'll have to agree, won't you, that it's possible for someone in the public relations field of political image-making to be honest and ethical and not be bent on duping the voters at any price?''

"I'd hate to debate you in front of an audience," Matt said, frowning. "You're very skilled at arguing your position."

"It's not that I'm so very skilled, it's that your position is so blindly stupid it takes very little to strike at it."

His frown deepened. "And somehow you manage to make me feel defensive when I know I'm right. You're very clever, Kayla."

Kayla groaned. "Obviously, I'm not clever enough to make a stubborn, prejudiced blockhead like you consider changing his mind, though. Is that what you came here to tell me—that I *am* what I *do?*"

Matt cleared his throat. "I came to tell you that I—I can't see you anymore, Kayla."

She had trained herself to expect the unexpected. In her field, anything could happen and often did. But occasionally, she was caught completely off guard. The night of Matt's fund-raiser had been one time. This was another.

"Let me get this straight," she said coldly, her hazel eyes flashing. "You came all the way over here, barging into my sister's apartment uninvited, to tell me that you can't see me anymore? When we weren't seeing each other to begin with? When I had no intention of ever seeing you again anyway?"

Put like that, it sounded ridiculous. He felt ridiculous. A slow flush crept from his neck to his cheeks. "I was trying to do the right thing. I felt I owed you an explanation," he murmured uneasily.

"You don't owe me anything! Get out of here." She gave him a hard shove. She couldn't remember ever being this infuriated, except perhaps the last time she was in Matt Minteer's presence.

"I couldn't just stop seeing you without a word," Matt protested. "I'm not the kind of guy who casually sleeps with a woman and never calls her again."

"So you decided to insult me in person, to dump me face-to-face!" Enraged, Kayla gave him another push toward the door. "How honorable!"

"I was trying to be honorable," Matt said desperately.

He was making a terrible mess of it, he conceded glumly. And no wonder. He'd been in frenzied conflict with himself since Kayla had announced that she was one of those heinous image-makers he'd always purported to despise. It stood to reason then, that he should despise her, too. But he didn't; he couldn't kid himself about that. All week he had been driving himself crazy trying to come to terms with his desire to pursue what he'd always loathed.

Finally, his cool, calm and controlled self had prevailed. Because he was a gentleman, an honorable man, instead of simply never bothering to see her again, he would do the gentlemanly, honorable thing and tell her why. After all, they had spent a night together and then he'd come on pretty strong to her at Bootleggers last week. She deserved an explanation....

Or so he'd thought. But her irate reaction indicated that he had gravely erred by coming here. He had ended up quarreling with her and had inadvertently insulted her. And now she was furious—he'd never seen anyone that mad! "Kayla, I'm sorry," he said, feeling frustrated and foolish and misunderstood.

His apology was not well received. "Oh, you're sorry, are you? Exactly what are you sorry for, Matt? Are you sorry that I'm not good enough for you? Sorry that I fall short of your impeccably high standards?" She put both hands on his chest, and using all her strength, gave him a forceful push at the same moment he tried to step aside to dodge her.

Neither of them saw the wooden magazine rack in his path. When he zigzagged to the left, his foot caught the side of it, and the momentum from her shove sent him flying off balance. Falling backward, he stretched out his arms, try-

FREE BOOKS CERTIFICATE

Yes! Please send me four **FREE** Silhouette Special Editions together with my **FREE** gifts. Please also reserve a special Reader Service subscription for me. If I decide to subscribe, I shall receive six superb new titles every month for just £11.10 postage and packing free. If I decide not to subscribe I shall write to you within 10 days. The free books and gifts will be mine to keep in any case. I understand that I am under no obligation whatsoever - I may cancel or suspend my subscription at any time simply by writing to you.

NAME

ADDRESS

POSTCODE

SIGNATURE

I am over 18 years of age.   **4S3SE**

A MYSTERY GIFT - **POST TODAY!**

We all love mysteries - so as well as the **FREE** books and cuddly teddy, we've an intriguing **FREE** gift for you.

Reader Service
FREEPOST
P.O. Box 236
Croydon
CR9 9EL

No stamp needed

MAILING PREFERENCE SERVICE

ing to grab on to something to stabilize him. However, the only thing within reach was Kayla herself.

When he caught her arms, she instinctively clutched at him and lost her own footing. They landed in a tangled heap on the floor, just inches away from Kristina's glass coffee table.

Winded and stunned by the tumble, they both lay silently for a moment or two. Kayla recovered first. After all, she'd had Matt to break her fall, landing on top of him. "You oaf!" she cried. "We almost crashed through the glass table. We could've been cut to pieces!"

Matt gingerly drew a breath. He'd hit the wood floor with his back and his head and both were throbbing. "You're the one who knocked me over." A humiliating admission; she was so much smaller but he'd gone down like a bowling pin.

"Well, you tackled me!" she accused indignantly.

"I did not. You lunged at me. Ouch." He disentangled his hand from beneath her hip to rub at his head. "Damn, that hurts."

Without thinking, she touched the spot he was rubbing. His hair felt thick and clean, her fingers tangled with his. "There might be the beginnings of a very small bump," she said tentatively.

"Small? It's swelling so fast, it'll be the size of a tennis ball soon." He swallowed hard. The pain was actually subsiding very quickly. The touch of her hand massaging his head was a blissfully healing balm. Their fingers collided again. The lump on his head might be swelling, but Matt was excruciatingly aware that something else, somewhere else, in his body definitely was. Given the intimacy of their positions, she had to be aware of it, too.

Their eyes met and held. Both were acutely conscious of the soft weight of her breasts pressing into the muscular breadth of his chest. They lay together, her atop him, stomach to stomach, thigh to thigh, loin to loin. And neither of them moved. They didn't dare.

"Kayla." He whispered her name in a husky, gravelly voice that sounded so sexy to her that a sharp glowing ache began to tighten deep inside her. A hungry fire blazed in his dark blue eyes.

His gaze electrified her. Her hands trembling, she skimmed her fingers over his high cheekbones, along the sharply defined line of his jaw. She was achingly aware of his burgeoning male arousal and a syrupy warmth flowed through her in response. She felt his arms come around her and it felt so natural, so right that she didn't even question it, let alone attempt to stop him.

"This is crazy," he growled. He was reeling from the instantaneous force of his desire for her, of his wild response to her. Why, why did he have to want her so much? He'd never been governed by sexual need; for years he had channeled his intensity and his energy into causes. No woman had ever come close to breaking the wall of self-control that guarded his passion—no woman until Kayla McClure. Who was everything he wanted and everything he despised combined. A tormenting paradox.

"I've been crazy since the night I met you," he groaned.

Kayla tried to think of a snappy comeback, a biting or funny remark to lessen the fiery sexual tension gripping them. But her mind went blank. She could only stare into his deep blue eyes, knowing that a corresponding hunger was reflected in her own.

It seemed inevitable. Their mouths came together with breathtaking impact. Her lips parted for his tongue that surged bold and insistent into her mouth. They kissed deeply, fiercely, possessively, again and again. Kayla clung to him, her nails digging into his back, her mouth ardent and tender under his. The heady passion erased all sense of time and place. Forgotten as well was the war she and Matt had been waging, their mutual vows to stay away from each other, to end whatever was between them before it could really begin.

Except that it had already begun, much as a spark smolders quietly and unnoticed until suddenly it blazes into a conflagration too strong and too wild to control.

Seven

Later that evening, as she drove back to Washington through a steady, heavy rainstorm, Kayla wondered what would have happened if, while ardently absorbed in one of those long deep kisses, they hadn't heard voices right outside the door, then the sound of a key being inserted into the lock. If she and Matt had been left alone for the evening, would those hungry kisses they'd shared have progressed into a full-fledged session of lovemaking?

Though it shamed her to admit, Kayla knew she wouldn't have stopped Matt from making love to her. She *couldn't* have stopped him. She'd been too far-gone, her common sense and her self-control overwhelmed by the raging needs Matt so effortlessly evoked in her. And from the intensity and force of his own responses, she doubted that he could have stopped, either. So it was a safe bet that she and Matt would have ended up in bed again—that is, if they'd made it that far and hadn't satisfied their tempestuous desires right there on the living-room floor.

A flash of heat streaked through her. Kayla shifted uncomfortably, clutching the steering wheel tightly. She dragged her mind from the tantalizing fantasy she was beginning to spin and thought about what had actually happened as she and Matt had lain together, wild and uninhibited, on that hard, wood floor.

Female voices, cheerful and laughing, had sounded through the door, and Kayla had instantly recognized one of them as her sister's. She pulled away from Matt and jumped to her feet, her body shaking with aroused desire and unmet needs.

"It's Kristina!" she'd exclaimed huskily, and Matt had groaned and slowly sat up, just as the front door opened.

Kristina and two other women came in. There stood Kayla, tousled and trembling, her mouth swollen from the ardent force of Matt's kisses while he sat on the floor, looking dazed, his blue eyes glazed.

"Oh dear," exclaimed Kristina in dismay. "I didn't mean to—I never thought that—" She exhaled and started over again. "You see, when I got to the restaurant, I realized that I'd forgotten my wallet. Wasn't that stupid of me? I forgot to put it in this bag when I changed purses tonight and so Lorraine and Diane and I decided to—"

"Kristina, you're babbling," Kayla interrupted softly.

"Well, can you blame me? I'm mortified! Kayla, Matt, I'm so sorry for barging in on you like this."

Matt rose slowly to his feet. Ever aware of implications, Kayla knew that he couldn't be happy to have three lobbyists find him in—well, not exactly in flagrante delicto, but sort of close to it. She felt compelled to offer him a way to save face, to smooth over the situation and put everybody at ease.

"You're not interrupting anything, Kristina. Matt tripped and nearly fractured his skull on your glass coffee table. Luckily, there was no harm done, but he...uh...needed a little time to regain his bearings."

Too late, Kayla saw the icy disapproval in his eyes and the sardonic smile twist his lips. She could almost read his mind: there she was, the image-maker at work, distorting the truth to control perceptions, a slick facile liar who couldn't even be honest with her own twin sister! *It isn't like that!* she wanted to protest. *I'm not like that!*

But Matt was already heading rapidly toward the door, as though he couldn't get out of there—and away from her?—fast enough. He turned, pausing long enough to bid a polite goodbye to Kristina and her friends. He didn't bother to even glance in Kayla's direction.

Kayla mumbled something about finishing her packing and hurried from the room, refusing invitations from the three other women to join them for dinner. She was out of the apartment and heading back to D.C. in record time.

And now here she was, driving in the rain on the dark interstate highway, a melancholy song about lost love playing softly on the radio. Scowling, Kayla turned it off and put in an audiocassette, a reading of a horrific, hair-raising murder mystery. It certainly fit her mood better than a love song. Love was a mystery she had to beware of and sex was a danger she didn't care to risk. As for Matt Minteer...

Kayla gulped. He seemed to personify it all, love and sex, mystery and danger. She'd made the vow before, but she made it again with determined fervor. She would not see him again, and if by some unfortunate coincidence, their paths happened to cross, she would not speak to him. She would certainly not come within touching distance of him or allow herself to be alone with him. She didn't dare take the chance.

It was a humiliating admission to have to make about a man who so patently loathed her, but Kayla faced it. As she often told her clients, one's weak points must be recognized and acknowledged before they could be modified or preferably, eradicated. For some cruel reason, fate had chosen Matt Minteer to be her weak point. Well, she had recognized it, she'd acknowledged it. Now she would eliminate him from her consciousness and from her life.

The month of March began with a raging snowstorm, inspiring weathermen everywhere to utter the "in like a lion" cliché. In keeping with the old conventional wisdom, they predicted the month would "go out like a lamb," with warm, pleasant weather. But that promise was no comfort to citizens experiencing a blizzard that dumped three feet of snow along most of the East Coast. Washington, D.C. was not spared.

Armed with a shovel and a few other essentials, Kayla wearily trudged outside to dig her car out of the parking lot...and fainted dead away in the middle of the job. When she came to a few woozy minutes later, she found herself sitting slumped in the snow, the ice scraper beside her.

She drew up her knees and laid her head against them. There was no reason to worry, she soothed herself. She'd been working strenuously in the snow for the better part of twenty minutes on an empty stomach. She'd been in a hurry to get the job done and hadn't bothered to eat anything that morning.

Yet another possible reason for her faint leaped to mind, as well. A nasty twenty-four-hour virus that was sweeping the city. Her assistant, Jolene, had caught it three days earlier and had returned to the office with a daunting tale of dizziness and nausea. Brightening, Kayla decided that she might have caught the bug from Jolene, because she certainly felt dizzy, and if not nauseated, then rather queasy.

It was one of those two conditions, either overexertion or sickness, that was the reason why she had fainted for the first time in her life. It had to be! Certainly, it had nothing to do with the fact that her period was a week late—for the first time in her life. A wild wave of panic assailed her. *She couldn't be pregnant!*

An image, clear and sharp, flashed in her mind's eye: Kayla saw herself sitting in her apartment after that crazy, abandoned and unprotected night of sex with Matt Minteer. Nature willing, she'd forget that night had ever happened, she had vowed to herself.

Well, she hadn't forgotten. She'd thought of Matt every day since, though he hadn't contacted her since his abrupt departure from Kristina's apartment that night several weeks earlier. Since her mind was unwilling to forget, suppose nature was unwilling to forget, as well? Suppose nature had conspired—*conceived!*—to leave a lasting reminder of that night? A gurgling, wiggling little bundle whose arrival could be dated nine months from that passionate night.

Kayla moaned aloud. *A baby!* What was she going to do if she was pregnant? She'd vowed never to speak to Matt Minteer again, and he had certainly made it easy for her to keep that pledge.

She had been in Harrisburg several times during the past month, and her presence in the city had been no secret. Twice she and Kristina had seen Luke Minteer and had exchanged perfunctory hellos, but there had been no attempts by Matt to see her or call her. Indeed, why should there be? He wanted nothing to do with her; he'd even made that special trip to Kristina's apartment to tell Kayla so—that same trip that had resulted in their passionate clinch on the floor!

Quickly, Kayla put that scene from her mind. She was successful in keeping thoughts of Matt at bay during the day. It was at night, when her defenses were weaker, that images of him slipped through, making her toss and turn, filling with a longing for something, for someone....

Kayla swiftly blocked those lonely nighttime yearnings, too. If only she could be as successful blocking them during the long, cold nights.

By the third week in March, Kayla noticed other subtle symptoms that couldn't be explained away by breakfastless exercise or convenient viruses. Her heart was in her throat as she slipped a pregnancy-testing kit into her shopping basket at the drugstore along with a few "cover" items. Back at home, she found that she didn't have the courage to even open the box of that fateful test, let alone make use of its contents.

Kayla ruefully recalled that she had been tagged the "independent twin," the braver, stronger sister, while she and Kristina were growing up. But right now, the independent, brave, strong Kayla, felt anything but. She needed someone she could trust and depend on, someone she could lean on.

A phone call to Kristina on a dismally overcast Sunday morning brought the twins together that same day. With Kristina's bolstering presence, Kayla administered the test.

"Oh, Kayla!" Kristina stared at the results, her eyes anxious and concerned. She read the instructions again, looked at the results again and exclaimed, "Oh, Kayla," several more times. Somehow, her genuine dismay helped. Already, Kayla felt less alone, stronger and braver. More like herself.

"Are you going to have it?" Kristina asked quietly, gripping Kayla's hand.

"Yes." Kayla blinked back the rush of tears that suddenly filled her eyes. "Even though part of me is scared to death, another part of me, a bigger part, is excited about having a baby. My own child! It'll be Mom and Dad's grandchild, a part of them living on all these years after they've gone."

"And you've always loved children," Kristina said thoughtfully. "I remember all those baby-sitting jobs you took as a teenager. I used to think that baby-sitting was a hideous form of torture but you never turned down a chance to do it."

"I know I can be a good mother, Kristina. I know I can handle a child mentally and emotionally and physically... it's financially that I'm worried about. My agency is taking in barely enough to cover my salary and Jolene's plus the overhead expenses. There's nothing left for advertising to promote the agency to draw in more clients, so I don't have any real hopes of expanding the business in the near future.''

"Remember what Penny always said?" Kristina stared into space. "'A pregnant woman is a dependent woman and no woman should depend on the capricious whims of a man for support.'"

Kayla grimaced. "Well, I don't need a man to support me and my baby. I'll do it myself. I'll manage on my own, Kristina."

"You don't have to, Kayla. You can depend on me—and Boyd, too. Move to Atlanta next month with me. After the wedding, you can live with us and have the baby and we'll all be one happy family."

"It's sweet of you to offer, but Boyd isn't going to want his pregnant sister-in-law living with him and his bride. Newlyweds need time alone, Kristina. Marriage is risky enough without starting out with an extra responsibility! Anyway, I do have a business to run here."

"Please think about it, Kayla. You know you'll always be welcome to stay with me."

"No matter how Boyd feels about it?"

"If he doesn't want to help my sister, then he's not the man I think he is and certainly not the man for me."

There, it was beginning already, Kayla thought grimly. Herself as a wedge between Kristina and Boyd. It wasn't fair! She would not let her own carelessness wreck her sister's chance at happiness.

"I won't change my mind. I'll be fine here in Washington, and we can visit back and forth." Because her sister looked so worried, Kayla hugged her and managed a wide, confident smile. "It's going to be all right, Kristina. If I painted too gloomy a scene, it's just because I'm...well, I'm still not quite used to the idea yet. But I will be. I'm not the first woman this has happened to and I won't be the last. The baby and I will manage. We'll even be happy, I promise. And I insist that you and Boyd be happy, too."

Kristina eyed her thoughtfully. "What about Matt Minteer?"

"What about him?" Kayla asked faintly.

"Kayla, he's the baby's father. The very least he owes you is child support—for the next eighteen years. And he seems to be the kind of man who would pay it, too."

"Oh yes, he's extremely honorable," Kayla said trenchantly. "I can attest to that."

Kristina didn't pick up on the sarcasm. "Yes, I think so, too. He has a reputation for honesty that's all too rare in politics today." She managed a smile. "Your financial situation won't be as bleak as you think, not with Matt helping you."

"Kristina, the day the lost continent of Atlantis rises from the sea is the day I'll mention this baby to Matt Minteer. This is *my* child. As far as I'm concerned, he has no rights or responsibilities toward it. He wouldn't want them, anyway," she added grimly. "Matt Minteer would view a child born to a political image-maker as something evilly akin to *The Omen*. Not to mention the fact that an illegitimate child could wreck his career."

"Mmm, not to mention that." Kristina looked thoughtful. "But what if you're wrong, Kayla?" she pressed. "Suppose he puts the baby ahead of his political reputation and acknowledges his responsibility to it? Then what? Is it fair to deprive your baby of its father? We grew up without our father and we missed him terribly, remember?"

"That was because we knew him and loved him until we were ten years old, Kristina. This baby won't know its father at all, and you can't miss what you've never had. You have to promise me you won't tell him, Kristina. *You have to promise!*"

"Don't get so upset, it can't be good for you. I—I promise."

"Swear it! You will not tell Matt Minteer about this baby!"

"I swear I won't tell Matt Minteer about the baby," Kristina repeated flatly.

Kristina returned to Harrisburg later that evening after countless assurances from Kayla that she was all right, that she didn't mind being alone, that she would call the moment she wanted her sister by her side.

The week passed slowly, with not much to do. Much of her work involved elections and none of her clients, except Elena, were running in the May and June primaries. Though she normally eschewed most of the industry socializing—all those dinners and small talk was Kristina's forte, not hers— Kayla did attend a broadcasting banquet that Thursday night. She wanted to hear the featured speaker, a legendary political speech writer, and he didn't disappoint his audience, entertaining them with stories and jokes for almost an hour.

She returned home shortly after ten o'clock and was parking her car in the nearby lot when she ran into Arlene Gallagher, who lived in the apartment on the first floor. They walked into the building together. "Kayla, I have the coffee I borrowed from you last week," said Arlene. "I'll run it up to you."

"Anytime, Arlene. There's no hurry," Kayla assured her. She'd read somewhere that caffeine wasn't good for pregnant women.

"I'll get the jar and be right up," promised Arlene. They joked about how their lives differed from those coffee commercials in which borrowing coffee led to romance. Not in this building, where there were only three unmarried men, two of them gay and living together, the third, a seventy-eight-year-old widower who kept steady company with a widowed lady friend.

Inside her apartment, Kayla leafed through a magazine and waited for Arlene. When the knock sounded, she rushed to open the door.

Arlene wasn't there with the proffered coffee.

"You!" Kayla gaped at Matt Minteer. He was wearing jeans and a navy sweatshirt and was leaning casually against the doorjamb. The navy color made his eyes look an even deeper, darker shade of blue.

Kayla's knees felt weak, but she made no move to step aside to let him in.

"Yeah, it's me." Matt didn't wait for the invitation he knew would not be forthcoming. He barged inside, causing her to jump aside with an indignant exclamation. "I...uh...drove down to check out the city. Thought I ought to familiarize myself with it since I'll be living here when my congressional term begins in January."

Kayla was nonplussed. "Isn't that a bit premature? It's only March, the primary hasn't been held yet and you haven't even won the nomination, let alone the election." She eyed him severely. "I've heard of confidence, in fact, I usually stress its importance in winning a campaign, but this is ridiculous!"

Matt shrugged. "I'm optimistic. And since I'm going to be moving here, I thought I'd better start scouting out places to live."

"You're not considering renting an apartment in this building?" Kayla was aghast at the notion, but swiftly masked her reaction. She was jumping to conclusions. It wasn't time to panic—yet.

"You wouldn't like it here," she assured him. "There are PR types all over the building—media coaches, political handlers, communications consultants on every floor." It was a slight exaggeration—well, a large one—but certainly justified under the circumstances.

He raised his dark eyebrows. "Sounds like you're trying to discourage me from moving in."

What game was he playing? "What do you want, Matt?" she demanded. Her stomach roiled, her palms already moist from tension. Calm down, Kayla scolded herself. He doesn't know; he couldn't. He was in town for political reasons and as she was such a ready target for his contempt, he had impulsively dropped by to hurl some more insults at her. Well, she'd let him and then he would be on his way, her secret still safe within her.

Matt hooked his thumbs into the belt of his jeans and looked at her. "Suppose I told you I'm here for some of your image-making expertise?"

Yes, he was definitely gearing up to insult her and her profession; that's all there was to it. Inordinately relieved, Kayla couldn't resist egging him on a bit. "You could benefit by it. I believe I told you that the national political scene, the one you'll be entering when you're a congressman on Capitol Hill, is different from local and state politics."

"Yes, you did tell me that. On the night we met, when you were pretending to be a lobbyist instead of a political communications consultant or handler or whatever it is you call yourself." He didn't take his eyes from her, and the piercing intensity glittering there made him look very dangerous indeed.

Kayla gulped. Suddenly she wasn't quite as sure of herself. But she rallied her defenses. This was her time and her territory and she wasn't going to meekly let him intimidate her. "Look, save yourself the effort of insulting me, I'm already well aware of your low opinion of me. You believe I have all the ethics of Dracula."

Matt firmed his lips into a tight, straight line. "I didn't come here to insult you, Kayla."

"I believe that as much as I believe that you actually came here seeking advice from me," she countered caustically.

There was a light knock. "Kayla? Here's your coffee," Arlene Gallagher called through the door.

Kayla went to get it. Fate was having a good laugh at her expense, she decided glumly. She'd never opened the door to anyone without first asking who was there, not until earlier tonight, when she hadn't had any doubt that it would be Arlene. And it had been Matt Minteer. Wasn't it Penny who said "Never trust a sure thing"? She was so right.

Kayla took the jar from her neighbor and closing the door, turned resignedly to Matt. "I was expecting Arlene in the first place," she said tartly. "If I'd known it was you, I wouldn't have opened the door."

Matt heaved a sigh. "Look, can we call a temporary cease-fire?"

"Why?" Kayla asked suspiciously.

"May I sit down?" Without waiting for an answer, he dropped down onto her blue-and-gray-striped love seat. "Kayla, I was thinking, you might be right about national politics differing from local and state politics," he said slowly, as if he was carefully choosing every word. He was watching her, his deep blue eyes fixed on her.

He was making her nervous, Kayla conceded. Very nervous indeed. "Exactly what is it you're trying to say, Matt?" she blurted out.

"There is one thing that remains the same in all levels of politics, though," Matt continued, ignoring her impatient interruption. "And that is the moral behavior and standards of the elected official. They must be beyond reproach."

"Or at least *appear* that way," Kayla said snidely. "Isn't that what we nasty image-makers are hired for? To cover up the sins of all those less-than-perfect politicians out there who want to dupe the unsuspecting public?"

Matt stood up. "You're not making this easy, Kayla," he gritted out.

"Oh, I'm so sorry," she replied with an exaggerated apologetic air. "If you'll tell me exactly what this idiocy is all about I'll try to be more accommodating . . . that is, as much as my devious, dishonest nature will permit, of course."

Matt took a deep breath, then let it out. "I know you're pregnant, Kayla."

Kayla gaped at him, immobilized by shock and horror. His revelation was so unexpected, a bolt out of the blue. Her mind reeling, she placed her hand against the wall to steady herself. "H-how—" she started to ask, then gasped the answer herself. "Kristina! She's the only other person who knew."

"She told my brother Luke. Took him to lunch today, then told him the news over the pasta salad. He told me immediately afterward, of course. I drove down here as soon as I could."

Kayla felt the color drain from her face. "You shouldn't have come."

He smiled crookedly. "Give me a break, Kayla. I wasn't about to sit at home watching the ball game on TV after hearing that news."

"Kristina shouldn't have done it! She promised she wouldn't tell you. She swore she wouldn't."

"She didn't tell me, not directly anyway. She told my brother." Matt shook his head. "Luke likes to view himself as unshockable, but he was shocked by this, all right."

"It was my secret! I know Kristina must've thought she was helping, but she had no right meddling in my life *again!*"

"You mean you weren't going to tell me?" Matt's voice rose. "Not ever?"

"That's correct," Kayla said tautly.

"For Godsakes, why not? It's my—mine, too."

"It's your what? Your problem? No, it isn't. I was care-less and I'll take full responsibility for myself and the con-sequences of my actions."

"It's my *child*," Matt corrected sharply. "And you weren't the only one who was careless. Hell, neither of us was intentionally careless, Kayla. If anyone is to blame, it's those WINDS maniacs for spiking everything we ate and drank that night. As for letting you take full responsibility, forget it. I'm going to take care of you and the baby. I won't have it any other way. We're getting married, Kayla. Right away."

"Have you lost your mind?" Kayla stared at him in dis-belief. "That's the craziest thing I've ever heard! We can't even pretend that we know or like each other! We spent one night together and neither of us were in full possession of our wits at the time!"

"We've been together more than that," insisted Matt.

"Oh, of course. There was our two-minute confronta-tion at Rillo's and the fifteen-minute one later that same night at Bootleggers. Those encounters certainly cemented our relationship, didn't they? And let's not forget those meaningful moments we shared when you appeared at Kristina's apartment uninvited, to tell me that you didn't ever want to see me again because my job didn't make me a woman of quality, that I wasn't worthy of your exalted presence."

A dark flush suffused Matt's neck and Kayla felt a mo-mentary sense of triumph. She'd scored a direct hit with that one.

"I didn't mean to sound so pompous or so arrogant that night," he said quietly. "What I said, my reasons for being there..." He paused. "It occurred to me afterward that I wanted an excuse to see you so I invented one."

"You wanted to see me, so the reason you invented to see me was to tell me you didn't want to see me anymore?" Kayla laughed. "What you're doing is what we in the in-

dustry call 'putting a positive spin' on a previously negative
incident. Too bad you disapprove of media consultants. You
certainly have the raw talent to be one.''

Matt's mouth tightened. ''What I'm trying to say is that
I regret what I said that night and I—I'm sorry I hurt you,
Kayla.''

''You didn't,'' she said quickly. ''For me to be hurt, I'd
have to care what you think of me and I don't. It's presumptuous of you to believe that you could ever hurt me!
You walked out of my life that night and haven't bothered
to see me or contact me since and I don't care a bit. I'm glad
you didn't. I didn't want to hear from you, I never think
about you...'' Her voice trailed off. The old saw about
''protesting too much'' was beginning to seem depressingly
apt.

''I thought about you, Kayla,'' he said quietly. ''Every
day.''

''Oh, spare me the hearts-and-flowers routine, if that's
what you're working up to. You feel guilty about the baby
and now you think you owe me some fairy tale about
yearning for me like a long-lost lover. Well, you don't, so
please save your storytelling skills for the voters.''

''You're really tough,'' he said.

Kayla thought she noted a grudging admiration in his
tone. No, she decided, it was just her foolish imagination
working overtime, spurred on by his ridiculous claim of secretly and silently wanting her all this time. She was horrified that she could be swayed, even momentarily, by such
insidious strategy.

She glared at him. ''Yes, I'm tough, and I don't need any
lying sweet talk from you.''

''You're right, you don't need lies from me. What you
need from me is my support and my understanding and my
loyalty. And a wedding ring, of course.''

A wave of exhaustion swept through her. He was so te-
nacious! Why didn't he just give up and leave? ''It's sin-

fully stupid for you and me to even mention the word *marriage,*" she said wearily. "We have nothing upon which to build a future together."

"We have a kid on the way, Kayla. That's a major cornerstone to build on, in my book."

"You're afraid it will tarnish your sterling reputation if word gets out that you're having a child out of wedlock!" Kayla accused. Hot angry tears stung her eyes. "What a hypocrite you are! You condemn so-called image-makers for what they do, but you're just as obsessed with keeping your own image untarnished, even to the point of offering to marry a woman you despise."

Before she realized what he intended, his big hands were cupping her shoulders. "This isn't about images, Kayla, not mine or yours or anybody else's. It's about a child. Our child. The one we made that night in the hotel. The one you're carrying inside you right now."

Tension and strength vibrating through him, he pulled her into his arms. Kayla felt the taut virile power of his arousal against her and gazed up at him with wide hazel eyes. He had barely touched her and yet...

"You shouldn't be surprised," he murmured huskily, reading her mind. "Just thinking about you makes me burn. And everytime I'm near you I get so hard so fast that I—"

"No, stop it!" Kayla tried to draw back. His words, his tone were undermining her resolve to resist him. "Let me go! This isn't going to solve anything!"

"I disagree. It proves that we're compatible in at least one major way. What you neglected to mention when you were reminiscing about our previous encounters is that they invariably ended like *this*."

His mouth opened over hers, drinking in any protest she might have made. His tongue thrust deeply and seductively into her mouth while his hands boldly shaped her body against his hard masculine frame.

Kayla stood passively in the circle of his arms for as long as her willpower held—which, to her shame, wasn't very long at all. And then, with a whimper, she gave in to the hot ribbons of sensation streaking through her. Slowly, in sexy feminine submission, she slid her arms around his neck and pulled him closer. Her mouth opened wider under his, and her tongue answered the hot demands of his.

Matt's breathing was becoming as rapid and shallow as hers. He moved against her, once again vividly demonstrating his swift, hard arousal. His hands moved boldly, possessively, over her, his fingers exploring the curves of her buttocks and hips, then the slender hollow of her waist before sliding upward to cup the soft weight of her breasts. He rubbed them through the yellow silk of her dress, fondling the softness with an expertise that made her moan. When his thumb unerringly found the ultrasensitive tip budding tautly, she cried aloud.

"Matt!" she whispered his name as she threaded her fingers through the dark springy thickness of his hair. His touch was burning her through the material of her dress and she knew a fierce, wanton longing to feel his fingers on her bare skin, to touch the hard naked warmth of him, to lie with him....

"It's such a risk," she murmured feverishly. "Such a risk."

"You've already taken it," Matt soothed. "We both have. The baby is a reality now."

He thought she was talking about lovemaking, but she wasn't, Kayla realized. She'd meant that loving was a risk. Did she dare take it?

There was no more time to think. They kissed and kissed, until she stopped worrying about all the reasons why this shouldn't be happening and let her emotions carry her, just as they had that first night she and Matt had been together. It seemed so inevitable, as if fate and nature had both combined forces to overcome all the barriers they had constructed to stay apart.

Matt muttered something dark and sexy under his breath and then lifted her in his arms. The sudden change in position made her head whirl. Kayla gulped for breath and instinctively clung to his shoulders.

Eight

In a few swift strides, he was in the bedroom. A pink light bulb glowed in the small bedside lamp, casting soft shadows over the room. Matt lowered Kayla onto the thick flowered comforter that covered the double bed and came down beside her, pulling her back into his arms and fastening his mouth on hers with a passionate urgency that matched her own.

The barrier of their clothing was an intolerable one that they tried to dispose of as quickly as possible. Matt tugged at the cloth-covered buttons of her dress, that stretched from the high collar to her waist. When they were finally opened, he pushed the material off her shoulders and swiftly dispensed with her yellow lace bra.

"You're beautiful, beautiful," he said hoarsely, and the rough desire in his voice made her feel sexy and voluptuous and utterly irresistible. It was the way Matt's immediate and hungry desire for her always made her feel, Kayla realized dizzily. He was the first and only man to make her feel that way, as if she were truly the only woman in the world who could assuage him.

"So pink and white and soft." His lips closed over her nipple, sensuously sucking it into his mouth. His tongue circled and laved the taut bud, and pleasure flowed through her like a wild, surging river.

A hot velvet blackness cloaked her, blocking out everything—common sense, the baby, their past antagonisms, everything that she'd used to keep away from him—and sent her spinning into a purely sensual realm where only the passion that burned between them was relevant.

She slipped her hands under his sweatshirt, reveling in the smooth flat warmth of his belly and the dark, curling hair on his chest. She loved to touch him, loved the feel of him, so male and hard and strong. Combing her fingers through the dark mat of hair, Kayla traced it downward where it disappeared into the waistband of his jeans. Through passion-slitted eyes, she saw the burgeoning distension behind the metal buttons of his jeans. Daringly, she closed her fingers around him.

Matt drew in a sharp breath and trembled at her intimate touch. "Easy, sweetheart," he said raspily. He reluctantly removed her hand and carried it to his mouth, pressing his lips to the center of her palm. "If you don't stop now, it'll be all over."

Kayla laughed shakily. "It's flattering of you to say so, but I'm hardly the type to induce an orgasm with merely a touch. Let's at least keep it honest between us."

"I am. And you definitely *are* the type. I'd let you prove it, but I don't want a quick—"

"My former fiancé proposed to another woman while he was still engaged to me," Kayla blurted out. "An experience like that tends to ground you in reality when it comes to assessing your own appeal."

"The guy was nuts to give you up," Matt growled. "*He* wasn't grounded in reality. Now it's time to stop talking about him. I don't want anyone else in bed with us, Kayla. There's only you and me here. No ghosts, no specters from the past. Just the two of us."

"There are three of us here now," Kayla whispered, catching his hand and placing it on her abdomen. An evocative, provocative action, to be sure, and she felt vaguely guilty for using their baby to further incite him, to bind him to her.

Why had she done such a thing when she'd been so adamant about his not even knowing about their child? If she ever came up with the answer to that, she could ponder an even more difficult question: Why was she making passionate love with a man she claimed she never wanted to see again?

"Oh, God, Kayla. I didn't think it was possible to want you more than before, but I do." His voice was thick with passion. "I've never wanted anyone more than I want you right now."

He swiftly, deftly pulled her dress over her hips and down her thighs, tossing it off with one smooth sweep. Remaining were her yellow bikini panties, which matched her bra and yellow-tinted stockings that ended at the top of her thighs.

Kayla's cheeks burned as Matt gazed at her appreciatively. "You look like one of those models in a lingerie catalog." He ran his finger around the yellow lace top of her right stocking. "How do you keep these things up, anyway?"

She explained that the lacy tops were elasticized and he slipped his fingers underneath to test. When they strayed to the soft skin of her inner thigh, Kayla felt electric tingles all through her. She caught her breath and shifted her legs. "How do you happen to be so familiar with lingerie catalogs, anyway?"

"I saw one at my sister's place," Matt confessed rather sheepishly. "I glanced through it and wow! it was as sexy as

Playboy. I wondered how I could get my name on the mailing list.''

She gave him a playful pinch. ''Are you one of those maniacs who slobbers over racy pictures?''

''Nope.'' He rolled over on top of her, letting her feel the full warm weight of him. ''Just a normal, red-blooded male who knows a good thing when he sees it.'' He buried his lips in the curve of her neck, tasting her skin. Inhaling, he smelled the sexy, womanly scent of her.

He knew a good thing and she was it, Matt thought, his head spinning. He was truly under her spell, but he couldn't seem to get alarmed about it. He knew he should, for her sensual power over him was intense and extreme. Yet at this moment, he couldn't even remember why he'd been determined to keep away from her.

Matt kissed her neck, then along her jawline until he reached her mouth. He took it hungrily, with unrestrained mastery.

Kayla lay beneath him, her arms wrapped tightly around him, her legs entangled with his, responding to his kiss with every fiber of her being. In a fog of sensuality, she vaguely recalled her resolute vow not to succumb to the chemistry between them again. It had seemed like a good idea at the time, and she'd had every intention of keeping him out of her life.

So much for vows and intentions, it seemed. Where were her much-heralded wits when she needed them? Her mind was as blurred as it had been during their first night together, but she had no alcohol-spiked excuse for it now, except that she wanted Matt Minteer with a fervid desperation that could not be denied.

They were kissing deeply as he hooked his thumbs into the waistband of her panties and stripped them from her. Her stockings were next; he smoothed them down along the shapely, silky length of her legs. Kayla shivered a little as she lay naked under his ardent gaze, not from cold but from the heat of his hungry, intense blue eyes.

"This is the first time I've really seen you," he marveled, almost to himself. "Last time it was so dark in that hotel room..." He stroked her skin, savoring its smooth softness as his eyes feasted on her generous curves. "I don't know how I managed to stay away from you for so long, Kayla."

"It's easy to stay away from someone you detest," Kayla said huskily, reaching up to caress the enticingly sensual lines of his mouth.

"I don't detest you, Kayla."

"Not at this particular moment anyway," Kayla murmured, drawing him down to her. She didn't want to argue the point or press the issue. Not now. Right now she *needed* to believe that he really didn't detest her, that he actually meant all the seductive things he was saying to her.

He slipped his hand between her thighs, seeking the throbbing feminine heat of her. His long, deft fingers caressed her, evoking spiraling waves of intimate, wonderful sensation. Kayla nearly sobbed as pleasure flooded through her; the remaining shreds of her control dissolved and she cried out his name, clinging to him.

Matt thought he might explode with raw desire. It took every bit of willpower he possessed to leave her long enough to pull off his clothes, but he couldn't keep away from her a second longer. *He had to be inside her!* With one powerful, deliberate thrust, he entered her. Locked together, they lay still for a few silent, sensuous moments.

He moved slowly, deeply, possessing her with a fierce passion that she returned in full measure. She moved with him and for him in erotic tandem, until they were both panting and breathless, their skin slick with sweat. Kayla gave herself to him completely; there were no reservations or inhibitions between them, no holding back. But even as they took, they gave to each other, their surrender as mutual as their sensuous demands.

And though they tried to prolong it, the wild, hot pleasure finally flared to flash point and the sweet flames engulfed them into a tumultuous, simultaneous climax.

Afterward, they lay in each other's arms, silent and replete in the afterglow. Kayla's eyelids began to feel heavy; it was an effort to keep them open. She shifted to her left side, her favorite position for falling asleep. Matt reached over to turn off the lamp, then tucked her into him, spoon-fashion, and draped a possessive arm around her. The lights in the living room, still on, shone dimly into the room. Matt considered getting up to turn them off, then reconsidered and didn't.

"Are you falling asleep on me?" he asked, stroking her hair lightly.

"I guess I am," she murmured drowsily. She didn't want to talk or think. She just wanted to float away on this sweet cloud engulfing her.

"Then now is probably a good time to ask if I can spend the night here."

"It probably is because I'm too tired to say no and face the argument you'll put up if I do."

"I left an overnight bag in my car." Matt pulled her closer. "But I'll get it later." He heaved a contented sigh. "This is great, isn't it? Not having to worry about birth control and protection and all that. I've always hated condoms and—"

"Don't press your luck, Matthew." She cut in sharply. "I said you could stay here tonight but I don't want an analysis of what is undoubtedly going to turn out to be a huge mistake on my part."

"It's not a mistake, but there'll be no analyses." He kissed her temple. "See how easy to get along with I can be?"

She had to laugh at that. "Oh, you're the soul of amiability, I'm sure."

This was, Kayla realized thoughtfully, the longest conversation they'd had without an exchange of angry words since their first night together. Did it mean anything other than the fact that they were good together in bed? There were lots of couples whose sexual relationship was dynamite but who were totally incompatible out of bed.

Penny immediately came to mind. Why, every relationship Penny had had, including her marriage to the twins' father, had been like that. Penny had warned her stepdaughters to beware of good sex: "It's merely a temporary smoke screen, not a solution to your problems. In fact, it can become your major problem."

Kayla could hear her stepmother's dire warnings as clearly as if she were in the room with them. She tried to put the troubling thoughts from her mind. She wanted to go to sleep, to forget everything for just a little while. Her eyelids closed heavily.

A moment later Matt's hand moved over the curve of her hip, then slipped to the dark springy delta between her thighs. Kayla's eyes flew open. She was suddenly wide awake again. And though she'd been limp with satisfaction from their earlier loving, she felt a fierce stab of response tightening in her groin, felt the moistness gathering there...

"Say you'll marry me," Matt said softly. Slowly, carefully, he turned her in his arms so she was facing him.

Kayla's eyes met his. Though the light in the room was dim, she was so close she could see his every feature—the intensity shining in his dark blue eyes, the unswerving determination that tightened his mouth. She swallowed. Instinct told her that a certain levity was definitely required. "Are you using sex to get your way?" she asked in what she hoped was a casually playful tone.

"I'll do whatever it takes, Kayla."

"Women are always being accused of controlling men with sex. It's considered unfair and manipulative, and now you're trying to do it to me."

Matt grinned rakishly, his blue eyes gleaming. "I already did it to you, sweetheart. But I'll be more than happy to do it again."

"If that's a double entendre, it's a dumb one," she began weakly.

"It's a promise, Kayla. Now tell me what I want to hear."

"What you want to hear," she repeated, closing her eyes. "That would undoubtedly be that I'm not pregnant, after all. Or that you're not the father. Or that I'm planning to have an abortion. You choose the one that most applies—*a, b,* or *c.*"

"How about none of the above? Marry me, Kayla."

She opened her eyes and looked into his. He had propped himself up on his elbow and was leaning over her, his expression intense.

"Why are you doing this, Matt?" she whispered, genuinely confused. "Why haven't you denied that you're the father? Why haven't you accused me of trying to stick you with some other man's mistake? At the very least, why haven't you offered to pay for an abortion?"

Matt laid his hand on her abdomen. "Jeez, Kayla, what kind of a man do you think I am? I was with you that night, remember? I know this baby is mine and we're going to get married and raise it, along with a few others." He smiled. "I like kids and I've always wanted them. I'm basically a family man, Kayla. I've stayed a bachelor for this long more by chance than by choice."

Kayla was flummoxed. This was far too easy; it was simply too good to be true. She was well aware that most single women did not get marriage proposals when they announced that they were pregnant. She knew from studying statistical analyses for various issue-oriented campaigns that there were many, many single mothers out there without men offering to take responsibility for the children they'd fathered. How many women became pregnant—either by accident or even deliberately in an attempt to push a reluctant boyfriend into marriage—only to be deserted and left to face the uncertain future alone? Far too many!

"A man doesn't propose to a woman he accidentally got pregnant," Kayla felt obliged to point out to him. "That sort of thing only happens in fairy tales—or romance novels."

Matt shrugged. "Well, I'm here and I'm proposing to you, and I've never seen myself as a Prince Charming or a romance-hero type. Say yes, Kayla."

"And if I do?" she asked warily.

"Then we get married and live happily ever after, of course."

"Just like a fairy tale." Kayla frowned. She felt as if she were trapped in a fractured fairy tale. Men and women didn't resolve their problems so swiftly; most of the time they didn't resolve them at all. She knew that from observing Penny and her men and from her own dismal experience with Scott Ceres.

She sat up abruptly. "My stepmother got pregnant by Don Felton, the man she married after my father. First, Don claimed that it couldn't be his child, then he offered her five thousand dollars to get rid of it."

Matt swore softly. "What did she do?"

"She took the money, used some of it to become a real estate agent and banked the rest. Don filed for divorce, relieved he wouldn't be stuck with a baby. She worked hard and eventually was quite successful. Owns her own agency now in southern California where she sells humongous mansions to the stars."

"With that incident in your past, I can see why you were apprehensive about telling me about the baby." Matt was silent for a long moment. "It occurs to me that I don't know anything about you, other than the fact that you have a twin sister who's a lobbyist and—"

"A career you consider odious," Kayla finished for him. "That's what I've been trying to tell you, Matt. We can't get married. We're strangers who—"

"Are going to get to know each other very well indeed. Except we'll do it after we're married rather than before, like one of those old-time arranged marriages. We'll make it work, Kayla. We can do it."

"You make me almost believe it can happen," Kayla said wryly. "With that kind of ability to sell yourself, I predict a long political career for you."

"I'll stay in politics as long as I can be an effective advocate for my constituents, but I'm not in it for lifetime job security. If I ever feel that I have to compromise my principles and beliefs, I'll resign from office."

"I feel like I'm listening to a sound bite I've written." Kayla slipped away from him and got out of bed. Her flowered silk robe was lying over the back of a nearby chair and she quickly pulled it on.

"A sound bite," Matt echoed flatly.

"Yes, you know, one of those short, catchy recorded statements that are short enough and catchy enough to fit into a twenty-second spot on the network news."

"I know exactly what a sound bite is and I also know that you're—"

"Your delivery is very good, and you get extra marks for that ring of sincerity in your voice," she cut in coolly.

"Nice try, baby, but it's not going to work."

She glanced at him. "What isn't?"

"I know you're trying to rile me with that cynical veneer. You sound like the political handler from hell. But I'm not buying the act, Kayla. I know how much you want me—you showed me everything I needed to know tonight in bed."

"Oh, did I?"

He nodded. "Right now the intensity of your feelings for me scares you, so you're putting on this hard-boiled con-

sultant act to try to drive me away. But I'm not going anywhere, baby.''

A cold streak of rage shot through her. Kayla pulled at the
lapels of her robe with trembling fingers. ''All right then.
You're welcome to stay right where you are. I, however, am
leaving. Good night.''

She stalked out of the room. Swift as a pouncing cat, Matt
caught her around the waist as she started down the small
hallway. ''Hey, was it something I said?'' Laughing, he
picked her up and carried her back into the bedroom.

Irate, Kayla did not join in the laughter. ''Put me down!''
she demanded. ''Was it something you said? Ohh! It was
everything that you said, you snake. You're insufferable.
Maybe I failed to drive you away, but you've succeeded in
driving *me* away with your insulting, preposterous arrogance.''

Despite her struggles, he handled her easily, putting her
back onto the bed with him. He wrapped his long limbs
around her and held her tight. ''Give up and relax, Kayla,''
he whispered against her ear. ''You're not going anywhere.
You're right where you belong, right where you want to be.''

''That is not true, you conceited, self-deluded—''

''Some sleazeball paid your mother to have an abortion
and then left her, so you expect all men to behave in the
same selfish way? Well, I have a news flash for you, honey.
They don't. *I* don't.''

''It wasn't my mother, it was my stepmother!'' Kayla
said, tight-lipped and furious. She was aware that her
struggles were futile against his greater strength, but she
didn't give up. ''You don't know anything about me so don't
try to pretend you do.''

''I want to know you, I want to understand you. Talk to
me, tell me—''

''No!''

"You might as well. I've figured out a few things already—that your parents are divorced and remarried." His tone was challenging, and Kayla reacted hotly.

"You don't have a clue! My parents were very happy together, they weren't divorced. My mother died of pneumonia when I was seven. My father married Penny, his secretary, a year and a half later. That marriage was a disaster. They could work together, but not live together. It lasted less than two years and then Penny contacted a lawyer about getting a divorce."

She swallowed hard, her rage suddenly dissolving. "The divorce never happened, though. My father was killed."

"Killed?" Matt echoed, shocked. "How?" His grip instinctively loosened as he turned her to face him.

"A car accident. It was late at night and he was alone and skidded off the road and into a tree. The police thought he'd probably fallen asleep at the wheel. Penny wasn't sure about that, though. She often wondered if he'd deliberately crashed just to get away from her without having to pay alimony."

"She told you that?" Matt gasped. "That's a helluva thing to say to a kid!"

He was temporarily distracted and Kayla knew she could get away from him. She could run down to Arlene's apartment. Her kindhearted neighbor would put her up for the night.

"God, you poor kid." Matt sounded genuinely disturbed. "Orphaned! What happened to you and Kristina afterward? Who raised you?"

He sounded genuinely interested, too. Kayla wasn't accustomed to that. In her line of work, all her clients were interested solely in themselves and their careers and what she could do for them. They never asked her personal questions; all that interested them about her life were her marketing and media skills.

His concern was irresistible. Unconsciously, she moved a little closer to him, but she stared into space, avoiding his probing blue eyes. "Kristina and I lived with Penny. She really didn't want us. She was only eighteen years older than us and she'd never had any desire to have kids. But there was nobody else who would take us."

"Nobody?" Matt asked incredulously. "No grandparents or aunts or uncles?"

"There was our mother's father and our dad's parents, but they said they were finished with raising children and couldn't take us. Dad's brother had three kids of his own and couldn't afford to take us. Kristina and I were grateful that Penny agreed to keep us. Otherwise, we would've been placed into foster care."

"And your own flesh and blood would've allowed that to happen? They couldn't afford to take you, they didn't want you—that's outrageous! Disgraceful! I've never heard of anything so heartless and selfish as turning your back on children in your own family!"

Kayla shrugged. "It wasn't so bad living with Penny. She was never mean to us or anything. Money was really, really tight for a long time, though. Penny couldn't afford to keep us, either, but she did it anyway. We went through two bad marriages with her—the one to Don Felton and then to another man, Anthony Abraxis. Neither lasted very long, not that Penny expected them to. Meanwhile, she kept working hard and by the time Kristina and I graduated from high school, she was doing very well. She insisted on paying our college tuition, and room and board, which she certainly didn't have to do. We're very grateful to her, we owe her, well, everything, really."

"That may be so, but she sure gave you some screwed-up ideas about men," Matt said perceptively. "I guess it's going to be up to me to revise them."

Kayla shook her head. "No, really, you don't owe me anything, Matt. If you insist on contributing to the baby's support, I will certainly accept whatever you choose to give but—"

"I choose to support my child and live with it and be its father in every way, Kayla. That includes staying married to its mother and providing a stable home."

A huge lump rose in her throat. "But I don't want to be foisted onto someone who doesn't want me. Not again, not at the age of twenty-eight," she cried.

"I want you." Matt's fingers tangled in her long, thick hair. "You can't possibly have any doubts on that score." He pulled her against the long, hard length of him, letting her feel the burgeoning throb of his very definite arousal. "I'll prove it to you again. Right now, if you feel you're up to it."

"That's just sex. We can't spend all our time in bed, you know."

"Don't underestimate the power of sex, Kayla. It's a powerful bond and we'll use it to forge a strong, permanent relationship."

"That sounds like singles-bar psychobabble. Next you'll ask my astrological sign and assure me that it's compatible with yours." She pushed at him with her hands and to her surprise, he let her go.

"Just to set the record straight, I've never asked about anyone's sign. It's sort of a point of pride for me." He rolled onto his stomach and closed his eyes. "You're tired and we've done enough tonight. Go to sleep, Kayla. We'll talk more in the morning."

She considered arguing. After all, she had a valid point to make—that a shotgun marriage between two people compatible only in bed augured nothing but trouble. But as a numbing fatigue seeped through her, the task of putting thought to words was simply too overwhelming. She was too tired even to take off her robe and put on a nightgown.

"In the morning," she mumbled, already drifting off to sleep.

* * *

Morning arrived with stunning speed. Matt awakened her with a hearty, "Time to get up. I'd like to be on the road within half an hour. We'll stop to eat breakfast along the way."

Kayla looked at him through half-slitted eyes. She didn't have the energy to open them all the way. "On the way to where?" she asked thickly. She felt stuporous and confused.

"Home," Matt replied briskly. "You need to pack a bag. We'll stay for the weekend."

It was still dark outside and the red numbers on her clock glowed an incredible 5:00 a.m.! And she was supposed to get up?

"You can't be serious," Kayla decided. She rolled over and snuggled deeper into the covers. Since he wasn't making any sense, she felt no obligation to listen any further.

"Okay, I'll pack for you. You can catch a few extra z's while I do. Ah, here's your suitcase, in the closet."

She heard him opening drawers and rummaging through them, then padding back and forth to her closet. Slowly, dazedly, she sat up and watched him tossing clothes—*her clothes!*—into her weekender case that lay open on the chair. "What are you doing?" she croaked.

"Packing your things for the trip."

Kayla was too exhausted, her mind too befuddled to comprehend more than one point at a time. Her tired brain never registered as far as "the trip," but she did pick up on the fact that he was packing for her.

"A man can't pack for a woman," she murmured sleepily. "God only knows what he'd bring for her. All the wrong things, that's for certain."

"Ah, sounds like another pearl of wisdom from the inestimable Penny. She seems to believe that a man can't do anything right." Matt tossed a black bra into the suitcase. "I used to know a soul mate of hers named Debra Wheeler."

He grimaced, then dropped a sleeveless white T-shirt into the case. "She too was of the all-men-are-either-idiots-or-evil-or-both school of thought."

Kayla blinked. "You just packed a black bra for me to wear with a white shirt. A sleeveless white shirt in March when we haven't had a day above fifty degrees yet."

"Should I pack you a sweater?" he asked solicitously.

"I'll do my own packing, thank you very much." She stumbled out of bed, threw out everything he'd put in the suitcase and started over. He had already carried her packed suitcase to the car, leaving her alone in the apartment for a while, when she was finally alert enough to recall, "What trip? We never discussed any trips."

"We're going to Johnstown to meet my family," said Matt. "Here, get dressed." He picked up some of the clothes that she'd discarded from the suitcase. A faded pink sweater she'd been meaning to get rid of for months and an old pair of aqua cotton shorts that was destined to become a dust rag. He tried to hand them to her.

Kayla shuddered and backed away. "I wouldn't wear that getup to sit alone in the dark in my own bedroom, let alone out in public. Besides, it's *cold* outside."

Matt heaved an exasperated sigh. "I guess I don't know anything about women's clothes. Pick out something yourself then."

"Don't worry, I intend to."

"And hurry up."

Feeling pressured, she snatched a pair of teal-green cotton leggings and a matching oversize tunic-length cotton knit shirt from the closet and fairly threw them on. Matt was hustling her out the door, even as she was stepping into her shoes.

It wasn't until they were both in Matt's car, pulling out of the parking lot when everything finally clicked. "Wait a minute, you tricked me!" Kayla exclaimed indignantly. "I had no intention of going anywhere with you."

Matt switched on the radio and kept on driving.

"This isn't fair! You woke me up at dawn, I was practically comatose and you took advantage to railroad me into this trip. Sleep deprivation is used to brainwash people, you know. And pregnant women need extra rest. I didn't fully realize what I was doing and now—"

Matt laughed. "I simply saved us both a lot of time, energy and arguing. You'd have ended up coming with me anyway."

"I want out! Turn this car around and take me home immediately."

"Sorry, angel. You're on your way to Johnstown to meet the Minteers."

Nine

"**R**elax." Matt reached over and took her hand in his. "There's nothing to be nervous about. My family will like you and you'll like them. They're not the ogres you're imagining them to be."

"I have no preconceived notions about them." Kayla pulled her hand away. His still rested in her lap and she lifted his wrist to place his fingers firmly on the wheel. "And I'm not nervous."

"Aren't you?"

"Not at all."

"You've been tying and untying the strap of your purse into knots for the past hundred miles," Matt said dryly. "Just doing it for the exercise, hmm?"

Kayla quickly dropped the strap that she was still unconsciously kneading with her fingers. "I didn't want to come with you, I don't want to meet your family and I'm not going to marry you. You can hardly blame me for feeling...uncomfortable about finding myself on this enforced trip with you."

"Ever been to Johnstown before?" Matt asked casually, completely ignoring the fact that she had just denounced him.

Kayla scowled. Much as she would've liked to ignore him, she felt obliged to respond to such a simple, direct question. "No," she said stiffly.

"It's a good, solid working-class town. It was badly hurt by the collapse of the steel industry in the early eighties, but it's still more bustling than most other western Pennsylvania towns. I guess the biggest, most uniquely defining thing about Johnstown is the Great Flood of 1889. It was one of the epic disasters of the nineteenth century with over twenty-two hundred dead or missing. It still casts its memory over the town. Each native Johnstown family has its tales of the flood, handed down from generation to generation."

"Does yours?" she asked. "Aside from that tall tale about Minteer's Tavern being swept down the river to Pittsburgh?"

"You remembered!" Matt smiled. "I remember how pleased I was that you laughed at my story that night. Most people don't laugh at my jokes. I'm not exactly known as a sidesplitting raconteur."

"You aren't one. I was merely being polite when I laughed."

"Nope, you really liked me, I could tell. You were as attracted to me as I was to you. And that was *before* our brains were blitzed by WINDS, Kayla."

She rolled her eyes heavenward. "You're quite good at recreating events to show yourself in a positive light. Are you sure you wouldn't consider working for Dillon and Ward? That's the sort of work they do for their clients, you know."

"Ah, Kayla, I know what you're doing. You're trying to inflame me by using all the buzzwords. But it's not going to work, baby. I'm not going to fly off the handle and call off our—uh—engagement."

Kayla winced. "We're not engaged. I was engaged once and it was a disaster. An engagement is so stressful...all that pressure, all those unrealistic expectations. Choosing a ring, seriously reading bridal magazines, all the artificial sentimentality and cloying jokes... Oh, I'll never go through *that* again!"

"I know what you mean. I was almost engaged once." He grimaced wryly. "It wasn't until Debra and I seriously started talking about marriage that I realized how wrong we were for each other. I couldn't have made a more unsuitable match if I'd deliberately gone out looking for one."

"Well, you certainly learned from your mistake, didn't you? This time you've decided to marry a stranger who got pregnant from a drunken one-night stand. *There's* a solid match for you."

"We're going to be a solid match," Matt insisted. "The more I get to know about you, the more I'm convinced we're right for each other."

His unshakable optimism astonished her. She'd never experienced anything like it. From childhood, she'd learned to be cautious, guarded, ready to be disappointed, to be wrong. "You're crazy," she breathed.

He shook his head. "Think about it, Kayla. We have the same values—you're loyal to your family—your sister and that wacky stepmother. You love them and are appreciative of them. It's that way with me and my family, too. Even more important, you want kids and so do I. You're willing to make sacrifices for your child's sake. You proved that by deciding to have our baby and to raise it, even before I entered the picture, despite the difficulties and inconveniences a single mother faces."

Kayla flushed. "You make me sound like some hallowed Mother Machree."

"I admire and respect you for putting the baby before yourself," he said warmly. "Our society has reached the point where it puts the individual's needs and rights ahead of the good of the family. People in other cultures are taught to be proud of making sacrifices for those they love, but that's not the case in ours these days."

She was at a loss for words. Hearing him state that she embodied those admirable, traditional virtues made her feel confident and proud and strong. How do you argue with someone who makes you feel that way? she wondered dizzily. Why would you even want to?

"We'll have a good marriage," Matt continued in those same riveting, mesmerizing tones. "Maybe we don't know each other as well as some couples do when they marry, but deepened trust and intimacy and commitment aren't just handed out on the wedding day, Kayla. They have to be developed and we're going to work at that every day."

He reached over and took her hand again, carrying it to rest on his thigh, their fingers interlaced. This time Kayla didn't pull away. She was bemused by him, confused by him, too. Everything in her life's experience told her that a relationship between the two of them was doomed to failure, that she shouldn't depend on him. But some spark of hope, so faint she was scarcely aware of it, flickered within her.

They rode with her hand in his through the mountainous Pennsylvania countryside. Kayla watched the road signs, saw the number of miles pass as they approached Johnstown. Her anxiety level increased.

"Johnstown sits in a deep valley in a gap in the Allegheny Mountains at the confluence of two rivers. You can see what easy prey the city is to flood waters," Matt said as they drove down the steep mountain road leading into the town below.

"Two rivers run down the mountains, the Little Cone-maugh from the east and the Stony Creek from the south, and meet at the bottom in Johnstown. With heavy rain, the two run wild, especially in the spring. The Signal Service—sort of a precursor to the National Weather Service—called the storm that triggered the Great Flood the most extensive rainfall of the century."

"I don't know much about the flood, but I seem to recall something about a dam bursting?"

Matt nodded grimly. "The South Fork Hunting and Fishing Club had an artificial lake made for the pleasure of their members, the coal and steel barons from Pittsburgh. The lake was fourteen miles above Johnstown and the dam that held it was known to be structurally faulty. When all that rain fell, the dam gave way and the water swept down the mountain with the force of Niagara Falls. Today, the U.S. Park Service operates The National Flood Memorial on the site of the club. The Johnstown Flood Museum is downtown and houses artifacts from the flood and runs daily showings of an Academy-award-winning documentary about it. We'll go to both places someday soon."

The morning was bright and sunny as they descended the mountain and Kayla tried to imagine it stormy and dark in a threatening downpour of rain, to picture the dam bursting and a lake full of water surging onto the unsuspecting town below. She shivered.

"Tell me your family's flood story," she said. "Was the Minteer Tavern really swept away?"

"It was flattened. There wasn't a piece of it left. My great-grandfather, Martin Minteer, was just a child of nine the year of the flood, but he could remember everything about it in stunning detail until the day he died. He told his son, my grandfather, all about it, and Pap passed on the story to every one of us. Martin described it so well you could al-most see it—a wall of water roaring down the mountains with trees and parts of houses and railroad ties, animal carcasses and all manner of debris in it, cascading along like a monstrous tidal wave, sweeping away everything in its path."

"He must have been terrified!" exclaimed Kayla.

Matt nodded solemnly. "He said it sounded like thunder, although others claimed the noise was more like an oncoming train. Martin and his parents and two little sisters were running to climb to higher ground with his father's brother and three cousins when it struck. Only Martin and his father and one fourteen-year-old cousin survived. The others were lost . . . swept away and drowned."

"Oh! That's terrible!" Kayla exclaimed. And even though the tragedy had happened over a hundred years ago to relatives he'd never known, she added a heartfelt, "I'm so sorry."

"Martin's father, my great-great-grandfather Patrick, was a tough old bird," said Matt with a proud smile. "He embodied the spirit of the city of Johnstown. He was determined to get on with his life, to rebuild, and he did. Within a year, the tavern was back in business, serving the workingmen of the Cambria Iron Company. In those days, the saloon was a place where the workingman could stop off at the end of a long shift to have a drink and socialize with his friends. He was always welcome there, even if he was covered with coal dust or sweat from the heat of the steel furnaces. It was his club, and on Saturday nights, things could get a little wild. Still does sometimes, although the excitement there these days usually comes from the football games playing on the large-screen TV."

"There's still a Minteer's Tavern, to this day," Kayla marveled. It was an interesting legacy, a continuity that her life had always lacked. Her baby's wouldn't; her baby would share the Minteer family history.

Kayla caught her breath. Did that mean that she was actually considering marrying Matt? This was the first time she'd acknowledged to herself that Matt Minteer had a part in her child's life, a role in both their futures.

Matt, unmindful of her internal upheaval, chatted on about Minteer's Tavern. "It's not as rough and rowdy as in the old days. Sometimes families come in for dinner, but after eight o'clock, it's pretty much a male club where sports and politics are always the hot topics of conversation. My brother Mark helps my dad and mom run the place. My brother John owns the local beer and soda pop distributorship. I worked in the tavern summers and school vacations till I graduated from college and I'll still pitch in and tend bar sometimes. For as long as I can remember the tavern has been a meeting place, a sort of pulse beat of local news and opinions."

"A natural political springboard," Kayla observed. "You know, I just realized something—you and your brothers are Matthew, Mark, Luke and John."

"We took a lot of kidding growing up because we weren't at all saintly like our namesakes. We're two years apart, with me the oldest. Two years after John came Anne Marie and two years after her, Mary Catherine. Then there was a five-year-gap and Tiffany was born."

"*Tiffany?* All those biblical names and then there is a *Tiffany?* Isn't that a bit modern?"

Matt chuckled. "Mom claimed a woman having her seventh child ought to be able to name it anything she wanted, and she was set on Tiffany. Tif's nineteen now, a college student at Penn State's Johnstown campus."

"I guess I'll be meeting her soon." Kayla gulped. "There certainly are a lot of Minteers."

"You'll soon be meeting them all," Matt said eagerly.

Kayla said nothing. She was suddenly very nervous about facing a multitude of Minteers in the role of... what? Exactly how did Matt plan to introduce her to them?

"You—you're not going to say anything to your family about the baby, are you?" She'd intended to sound authoritative; instead, much to her consternation, she sounded pleading.

"Not if you'd rather I didn't," Matt said soothingly. "We can tell them later."

"What about Luke? Do you think he might've told them already?"

Matt frowned. "Not a chance."

They drove through the city streets to a residential neighborhood where big, old brick houses lined the streets. "Here's the old homestead," Matt said fondly, pulling alongside the curb of a three-story red brick house. "We all grew up in this house, but only Mom, Dad and Tiffany live here now. Everybody else is married and lives in the suburbs with their own families, except Luke and me, of course. We live in Harrisburg, but we also own a duplex a few blocks from here. Each of us has his own side, which makes it a safe arrangement." He smiled ruefully. "You never know what Luke might be up to... or at what time. He can be a very nocturnal animal."

Matt took her arm to help her out of the car. Kayla felt an overwhelming urge to remain right where she was. Slowly, her eyes wide, her stomach churning, she walked to the front door of the big old house, Matt's arm clamped around her waist. To onlookers, it would appear that he was being solicitous and devoted. Kayla knew he was imprisoning her so she couldn't take off and run.

To her surprise, the Minteers, a group of countless men, women and children of all ages, were gathered at the house and obviously expecting her.

"Matt called from Harrisburg yesterday to tell us you were coming," said Rosemary Minteer, Matt's mother. "It was short notice but everybody is here, from Gram and Pap right down to little Ashley." She beamed at her youngest grandchild, three-month-old Ashley Minteer. "We're so excited to meet you at last, Kayla." Impulsively, she swept Kayla into a warm hug.

"At last?" Anne Marie, the oldest sister, repeated, arching her eyebrows. She juggled a squirming two-year-old on her hip. "We didn't know of her existence until yesterday, Mother."

Anne Marie turned to Matt, eyeing him severely. "Matthew, I can't believe you've been secretly dating her and never bothered to bring her home until now." With her free hand, she gave his arm a sisterly punch. "Kayla must've been wondering why you didn't introduce her to your family long before this! That's just not the way it's done."

"Hey, I wanted to surprise you, Annie. You're always saying I'm too controlled—now you're complaining because I'm being spontaneous."

Grinning unashamedly, Matt clamped his hand around the nape of Kayla's neck and guided her out of the crowded vestibule into an even more crowded living room. "Anne Marie has an opinion on everything and she's not shy about sharing it."

Kayla was not concerned about his outspoken sister, she was still reeling from his mother's remark. "You called *yesterday* from Harrisburg to tell them we were coming?" She stood on tiptoe to murmur in his ear in a low, fierce voice that no one but him could hear. To the curious, fond onlookers they appeared to be lovers sharing a private word. "Yesterday, *before* you came to see me in D.C.?" A tremor shook her. "Where you then proceeded to seduce me and then steamroller me into coming with you!"

In turn, Matt leaned down and whispered in her ear, "I plead guilty to the steamroller charge, but the seduction was definitely mutual."

"Matt, Kayla, smile!" someone with a video camera shouted.

"Look this way," called another person with another video camera.

"I want to see the ring," demanded someone else.

"There is no ring," Matt said jovially. "We both hate engagements and everything to do with them, so we're skipping all that and going directly to the wedding ceremony."

"Everything's fixed, Matty, my boy." An older man slapped Matt's shoulder. "All you have to do is go down to the hospital for the blood test. Judge MacClaren worked a little magic and got you the license." He reached into the pocket of his jacket. "It's right here."

Matt grinned. "Thanks, Uncle Mike."

Kayla glimpsed the notarized piece of paper as Matt took it from his uncle. The words swam before her eyes. It was, unmistakably, a marriage license.

"The church is reserved and Mary Catherine's brother-in-law, Father Aaron, is going to officiate," said Jack Minteer, Matt's father.

"I hope that's all right with you, Kayla," Mary Catherine said. "My husband, Ed's, older brother is a priest, and he officiates at all our family services. I guess we never thought to ask if there was someone you wanted to perform the ceremony."

Kayla cleared her throat. It seemed imperative that she make some comment, but things were moving too fast for her to fully comprehend them. From the clues she'd seen and heard—the marriage license, the talk about a church and priest and ceremony—it was clear that something was afoot. But a wedding? That just couldn't be! Apprehensively, she looked up at Matt with questioning hazel eyes.

"Father Aaron is fine, Sis," he said, holding Kayla's gaze. "What time is the wedding scheduled?"

"This afternoon at four," Anne Marie informed them. "You certainly didn't give us much advance notice, Matt. I barely had time to run over to the mall in Altoona to get a new dress and shoes for me and new outfits for the kids."

"But she did it. Anne Marie can always make a shopping deadline," her husband chimed in cheerfully.

Kayla's legs nearly buckled. If Matt hadn't been gripping her firmly around the waist, she probably would have collapsed to the floor. "But—but—" she began, her voice shaking with shock. The Minteers had arranged for her to marry Matt today at four? She stared wildly around her. There seemed to be hundreds of them crowded in the house, blocking the entrances, preventing her escape.

"Are you worried that Kristina might not be able to make it by then?" Matt asked in a perfectly natural tone of voice, as if they'd discussed all this before, as if Kristina's appearance was the only thing that might be troubling her. For a minute, Kayla wondered if she were losing her mind.

"Kayla and Kristina are identical twins," Matt explained to the relatives pressed around them, listening. "I bet you'll have trouble telling them apart. I know I've had my share of mixed-up moments," he added dryly.

"Don't worry, sweetheart," he said, turning to Kayla with a heart-melting smile. "Kristina is driving down from Harrisburg today, and bringing your dress, of course. She should be here by one."

Kristina was in on this, too? Her own sister had conspired with the Minteers to marry her off to Matt today? Kayla was speechless with shock; an aura of unreality enveloped her. One event was following another with dizzying speed and she had no control, no options. She felt a vague connection to the hapless flood victims, trapped before that overpowering fateful deluge.

"Well, look who's here! Luke, you made it!" exclaimed Mark, greeting his brother with characteristic Minteer exuberance.

"Of course I made it. I wouldn't miss Matt's wedding for anything—or anyone, no matter how alluring," Luke added suggestively. The brothers laughed.

Luke looked directly at Kayla and though he was smiling, she could sense the animosity in him. She knew she wasn't imagining it, and when he cornered her alone in the kitchen a short while later, the coldness in his blue eyes confirmed his hostility. He made no pretense of smiling now.

"Well, you did it," he said in a low growl, out of earshot of the children gathered by the refrigerator, clamoring for drinks. "You successfully trapped my brother. You knew damn well that he would never let his child be born illegitimate."

"I—*trapped*—" Kayla was incredulous. "Are you suggesting that I deliberately planned this to make Matt marry me?"

"It's the oldest trick in the book and I can't believe Matt fell for it. You knew my brother had a severe case of the hots for you and you took full advantage. You seduced him while conveniently forgetting the birth control. Bingo. You're getting a ring on your finger. You've hooked up with a political rising star with a limitless future and—"

"You couldn't be more wrong!" Kayla cut in hotly. Luke saw his brother as the innocent victim of her treacherous wiles? If he only knew that *she* was the one being trapped into this marriage by his own family!

"Have you forgotten that *you're* the one who told Matt about the baby, after Kristina told you," she whispered crossly. "Why didn't you simply keep the information to yourself? Matt would have never known and—"

"Don't even try to use that one! You know damn well that your sister gave me an ultimatum. She said if I didn't tell Matt immediately, she would. And she would also tell him that I'd tried to keep the news from him. You both knew Matt would never forgive me for that. So you win—for now, babe. But I'll be watching you and if you dare to—"

"Here you are!" Rosemary Minteer joined them in the middle of Luke's threat. "Luke, now that Matt is getting married, I hope you'll feel sufficiently pressured to settle down, too. You've wasted enough time dating and partying."

"Yeah, Ma. If only I could find a sweet girl like Kayla, maybe I would," Luke said with credible sincerity. He and Kayla glared at each other, but Rosemary remained oblivious to the tension.

Matt joined them at that moment, glancing from Kayla's pale face to Luke's flushed one. He frowned and put a protective arm around Kayla's waist.

Rosemary Minteer enfolded both Matt and Kayla in an emotional embrace. "I'm so thrilled about this wedding. So happy for you both!"

What was she going to do? Kayla wondered wildly. There were so many Minteers and they all seemed to be talking at once. She found their ebullience almost as unnerving as Luke's hostility. Should she let out a piercing scream? That might get their attention long enough for her to be heard. She would tell them that she was *not* marrying Matt....

Simply visualizing the scene paralyzed her. What would they do? Suppose the mood turned ugly? Luke had already tacitly threatened her. What did she know about these people anyway?

"Matt, I brought your suitcases in from the car." His brother John appeared with the two cases, hers and Matt's. "Want me to carry them upstairs?"

"Yeah, put them in my old room," instructed Matt. "Kayla wants to go up and freshen up before we leave for the hospital for the blood test, don't you, sweetheart?"

She nodded dumbly and allowed him to lead her up two flights of stairs to a small bedroom at the end of the long hall. While Matt and John chatted, she walked to the window and looked out. It was at least a thirty-foot drop to the ground and the closest tree was not near enough for her to reach it and climb down. So much for that rather theatrical mode of escape.

"I'll leave you two alone now, but remember, there's a houseful of relatives downstairs who will start speculating on what you're doing if you stay up here too long." John winked at Kayla. "We Minteers are notorious about minding one another's business."

Kayla did not wink back. She was too horrified.

Matt gave his brother a comradely pat and sent him on his way. The moment they were finally alone, Kayla turned on him like a virago.

"Wedding? This afternoon? Have you gone crazy? How could you? How dare you? You—you practically kidnapped me and now you intend to—to marry me against my will?"

Matt closed the bedroom door and stood in front of it, unyielding and inexorable. "I know it's a...er...shock, but Kristina and I decided that it was for the best, Kayla."

"Kristina and you decided?" she echoed. Her sister was more deeply involved than she'd ever suspected; she'd actually instigated this, along with Matt himself. A wave of depression crashed over her. She felt abandoned and alone.

"Kristina is worried sick about you, Kayla. She was terrified that you'd insist on cutting me off completely and going through the pregnancy alone. And—"

"She had no right conspiring with you against me!" Kayla cried. "It's *my* decision, *my* choice to make. And if I chose to go it alone, then—"

"If you were the only one affected, I might agree," Matt cut in roughly. "But there's a baby to be considered, Kayla. And that baby has a right to both parents. I want my child, Kayla, and I intend to be married to its mother when it's born."

"I'm the one having it! It's mine!"

"And mine, too. Okay, I admit that having my family arrange this surprise wedding might be a bit highhanded—"

"A bit? Try *incredibly* high-handed! Despicably arrogant. Shamefully presumptuous!"

Matt sighed. "I get the picture. But, let's face it, Kayla, you're going to marry me, sooner or later, we both know that. I suppose I could've gone through the motions of a courtship but it would have been damned inconvenient with you living in Washington and me in Harrisburg and you getting bigger with the baby every day. And you're certainly stubborn enough to wait until you're being wheeled into the delivery room before finally accepting my proposal. I'm not good at that kind of melodrama, Kayla. I couldn't handle it."

"Who says I'd have married you sooner or later?" Kayla wearily sank onto the narrow single bed against the window. "How can you presume to know that?" The burst of anger left her feeling drained and exhausted. She needed time alone to recharge herself for their next round.

Matt didn't give it to her. "You can chalk it up to my monumental overconfidence," he said lightly. "Or my despicable arrogance. Or maybe my shameful presumptuousness. Your choice." He glanced at his watch. "It's time to leave for the hospital. Do you want to...uh...use the facilities first?"

He showed her where the bathroom was and Kayla locked herself inside. A quick check out the window—the same steep drop and distance from the tree—also ruled it out as an escape route. Miserably, she paced the floor, her thoughts chaotic.

Matt rapped on the door ten minutes later. "Ready, Kayla?"

"I'm staying in here," she announced.

A girlish giggle sounded outside the door. "I don't blame you, Kayla," came an unfamiliar feminine voice. "I used to lock myself in the bathroom to escape from my relatives, too."

"Tiffany's here," Matt explained through the door. "Come out and meet her, Kayla. She's riding along to the hospital with us."

"Bringing her along for protection?" Kayla snapped. "It won't work, Matt. Whatever I have to say to you, I'll gladly say in front of your little sister."

"Call me psychic, but I think I sense some tension between you two," said Tiffany. "You've had a fight, huh? Suffering from pre-wedding jitters or something?"

"Something like that," said Matt. "Kayla, I can take the door off the hinges if you won't open it, but do you really want to go through all that?"

No, she really didn't. Kayla imagined a horde of Minteers crowded around him, cheering him on while she hovered inside. She flung open the door. Matt was lounging against the wall. The young woman standing beside him, rocking back and forth on her heels, was nearly six feet tall, long-limbed and lanky in jeans and a sweatshirt.

Matt smiled at Kayla. "I'm glad you decided to be reasonable, honey. Meet Tiffany, my baby sister, Tif, this is Kayla."

"Hi, Kayla. Welcome to the family," Tiffany said cheerfully. "I volunteered to drive you two to the hospital for the blood test so you could sit in the back seat and neck on the way."

Before Kayla could reply, Matt draped one arm around her shoulder and the other around Tiffany's. "Let's slip out the back and escape all the commotion."

Kayla was so glad to get away from the crowd in the house that she made no protest.

Not surprisingly, Matt and Kayla did not neck on the way to the hospital. Nor did they argue. Instead, they sat, politely restrained in the back seat, while Tiffany talked and talked on a wide range of subjects. Kayla was somewhat awed by her loquaciousness. She worked with politicians, a group never known for their reserve, yet she'd never heard anyone talk as incessantly as Tiffany Minteer.

"Everybody in the family was stunned when you called yesterday and asked them to set up your wedding," Tiffany chattered on as the three of them traipsed into the hospital lab. "They couldn't picture Matt, of all people, having a whirlwind romance but I myself believe in love at first sight. I think it's a past-life sort of thing."

"Not that again!" Matt groaned. "Tiffany thinks we've all lived before. In fact, she firmly believes we were living in Johnstown back in 1889 and were wiped out in the flood."

"It's true, I do believe that," Tiffany said seriously. "I've never liked swimming. And remember how I hated to get my face wet when I was little? Why, even getting a shampoo was traumatic for me, a vestige from my tragic end in my past life."

"I guess it couldn't have been something as simple as getting soap in your eyes and feeling it burn, huh, Tif?" Matt asked, a trifle sarcastically.

Tiffany was undaunted. "Well, how about the way you and Kayla instantly connected?" she persisted. "You told Mom you met her and knew immediately you wanted to marry her as soon as possible. It's obvious to me that you two shared a past life together. Maybe you were lovers who drowned in the flood, holding on to each other as you were swept under the water."

Matt heaved a sigh. "You've seen those flood movies too many times, Tif."

Kayla made no comment. At this point, Tiffany's reincarnation theory struck her as no more bizarre than the rest of this strange day.

She watched impassively as the lab technician filled a vial with her blood, although the test was more of a formality than a necessity since the marriage license had been obtained by a special judicial favor. Part of her wondered at her peculiar passivity. Was she going to simply allow the Minteers to hustle her to the altar? Time was running out; there were only a few more hours until four o'clock.

Kristina had already arrived at the Minteer house when Matt, Kayla and Tiffany returned from the hospital. Kayla took one look at her sister, who was sitting in the dining room with a plate heaped with food, and suddenly emerged from the dazed inertia gripping her.

"May I see you alone, Kristina?" she asked very sweetly. "Upstairs, please?"

"Going to talk strategy?" Luke's tones were as saccharine as hers. "You sisters work so well together as a team. You're on a real winning streak, too."

"There will always be winners and losers," Kristina said, smiling fixedly. "Which group do you belong in, Luke?"

Matt had been spirited into the kitchen by an aunt, so his brother John walked the twins upstairs to the spare bedroom on the second floor where Kristina's luggage had been deposited. An ivory-colored suit in a dry-cleaners bag was hanging on the outside of the closet door, a pair of matching high-heeled pumps were in an open shoe box on the floor.

"Kristina tells me you're wearing that for the wedding," John said amiably, nodding toward the suit. "It's really pretty, Kayla."

"I didn't know what color blouse you wanted to wear with it, so I brought you a choice of five, Kayla," Kristina said nervously, opening the closet door. "There's hot-pink, royal blue, bright yellow, pumpkin or olive."

John drifted away, leaving the sisters alone.

"So which color will it be?" Kristina asked. She fiddled with the blouses, nervously chattering on, her eyes avoiding Kayla's. "Uh, what do you think of the Minteers? I like them all except brother Luke. Oh, isn't he obnoxious? He's been making snide little jibes ever since I arrived and—"

"I don't want to talk about Luke. My problem is with *you!* Kristina, how could you?"

"Please don't be mad, Kayla," Kristina interrupted quickly. "At least not *too* mad. You know I only did it for you...and for the baby, too, of course. That's my very first niece or nephew you're carrying, you know."

"I don't want to hear any of your rationalizations, Kristina! You told Matt about the baby against my expressed wishes. And don't try to con me with that Luke loophole—you knew he'd tell his brother! You assured it. Now you've conspired to trap me into this wedding to a man whom I—"

"If you don't want to marry him, then don't," Kristina interjected sharply.

Kayla gaped at her. That was probably the last thing she'd expected her sister to say.

"No one is holding a gun to your head, Kayla," Kristina continued. "If you're determined not to marry Matt, then let's go downstairs and tell everybody the wedding is off."

Kayla was staggered. She imagined walking downstairs and standing amid all those smiling faces and telling them....

"I—I can't do that, Kristina," she blurted out.

"Of course you can. I'll go with you, if you'd like. Just say you've changed your mind and we'll be on our way. My car is parked right out front and I'll drive you back to Washington. Nobody will keep you here against your will, Kayla. No one is going to drag you into that church and make you say 'I do.'"

Kristina was right, of course. The full implication of that revelation hit Kayla with stunning force. Granted, it would be unnerving, but she could walk out of here any time she wanted, without going through with the wedding.

Kayla's mouth was suddenly very dry. She could hardly swallow. "But—but Matt is—" she paused to wet her lips with the tip of her tongue "—it would be humiliating for him to be dumped so publicly. His whole family is expecting us to get married, they've made all these plans for the wedding and they—"

"What do you care if Matt is humiliated or his family is disappointed?" Kristina cut in.

"Well, I—I—know how it feels to be rejected. Remember when Scott Ceres broke up with me and immediately got engaged to that conniving Victoria Dillon? Imagine how Matt would feel if I left him, with his whole family looking on, believing we're in love and that he's going to marry me! I—I just couldn't hurt him that way."

"So you're willing to marry Matt because you feel sorry for him?" Kristina laughed incredulously.

"Of course not! I'd never marry a man out of pity!"

"I'm not following your argument, Kayla. Are you going to marry him or not?"

Kayla stared at her. "Oh, Kristina, I—I think I am."

"You mean it? You really mean it? You're not just giving in to pressure or exhaustion or—"

"I mean it," Kayla said, and this time she wasn't astonished by her own admission. "Kristina, I'd like to be alone for a while...to get dressed and...and to think things over."

"I'll go back downstairs and finish eating. Those Minteers can really cook!" Kristina gave her a swift hug. "You made the right decision, Kayla."

Yes, she had. Alone in the room, Kayla finally felt in full control of herself. And as a thinking, mature woman, she realized that marrying Matt Minteer was the best thing to do all around.

Now if she could just get through the wedding...

Ten
___

Minteers of all ages exuberantly congratulated themselves that the impromptu wedding had "gone without a hitch." Almost everybody had had a hand in arranging the event and locating such wedding staples as the organist, flowers for the altar, Kayla's bouquet and even a multitiered cake in a mere twenty-four-hour time span. After the ceremony, a celebratory reception was held in Minteer's Tavern, which was to be temporarily closed to the public until after the departure of the newlyweds.

Kayla, in Kristina's cream-colored suit and royal blue blouse, was thankful for the Minteer ebullience, because it relieved her of having to do anything but smile and nod during the noisy celebration. Someone fixed her a plate from the buffet table that offered a feast of traditional west Pennsylvania wedding food—an ethnic mix of pierogi, rigatoni, chicken legs, chipped ham, mounds of potato salad and countless plates of cookies. Kayla made a pretense of eating, desultorily moving the food around with a fork. Like many a bride on her wedding day, she was too nervous to eat.

However, unlike most brides, she had married a man she had never had a date with. They'd skipped such traditional rites as the first phone call and the first date and moved directly to marriage and impending parenthood.

Matt stayed by her side during most of the festivities, and from time to time, Kayla would stare at him, masculinely resplendent in his dark blue suit and white shirt, and try to assimilate the fact that he was her husband. It didn't seem real, though the plain gold wedding band encircling her third finger, left hand, proclaimed her new status as a married woman. Yes, the Minteers had even come up with matching wedding rings for her and Matt.

By nine o'clock, couples with young children began to depart, and Matt's father and brother Mark jokingly announced that the reception was over and their paying customers were now being admitted.

A group of regulars streamed into the bar and were immediately treated to a round of celebratory drinks on the house. While Matt was being heartily congratulated by the patrons, each of whom he knew by name, Kayla slipped into the women's bathroom. Kristina pushed her way into the closet-sized room with her before Kayla could lock the door.

"You look tired," Kristina said bluntly, as Kayla half-heartedly tried to rub off all the lipstick prints marking her cheeks, the result of many kisses from many relatives.

"I think shell-shocked is more like it." Kayla glanced at the shiny new wedding band, remembering the moment Matt had slipped it on her finger. A small shiver tingled along her spine as she recalled the intensity burning in his eyes. "Looks like I married a politician, in spite of our pledge never to get involved with one."

"It was a stupid, unrealistic pledge," said Kristina. "As stupid and unrealistic as Matt's belief that all political consultants are jackals. You are two unique people who can't be stereotyped.''

"Spoken with the customary lobbyist finesse.''

"Kayla, please try to understand.'' Kristina took both Kayla's hands in hers and held them tight. "I didn't want you to make the same mistake that I made with Boyd two years ago. I was afraid to trust him or myself enough to make a commitment and I drove him away. I sensed you were going to do that to Matt, and that's why I interfered. I spent two of the most miserable years of my life, regretting my breakup with Boyd before I finally admitted my mistake. But with the baby coming, you can't afford to wait years. I had to act. *We* had to act!''

Kayla resumed trying to repair her makeup. She'd tried to stay angry with Kristina, but couldn't. Her actions were her own responsibility and foisting the blame on her sister was unfair.

The twins' eyes connected in the mirror and Kayla smiled wryly. "But since you helped to engineer this wedding, I'll let you call Penny and tell her about it. I'm not up to listening to her moan because I didn't get an ironclad prenuptial agreement signed before the ceremony.''

Kristina's eyes gleamed. "I'll tell her she's going to be a grandmother. I can almost hear her amend that to *step*-grandmother. And then she'll go into her 'I'm only a few years older than you girls, certainly not old enough to be your mother' spiel.''

"And certainly not old enough to be Grandma.'' Kayla grinned in spite of herself. "Penny ages in reverse—she's soon going to be younger than we are.''

"She's sure different from Matt's mother,'' observed Kristina. "And from the other women I met here today. All the Minteers are different from our relatives, Kayla. If any of the kids in that family were orphaned, there would be a whole slew of people eager to take them.'' Her eyes met

Kayla's in the mirror. "Your baby will have that security, Kayla. It's something we never had."

"I know," Kayla said quietly. "I guess that's part of the reason why I . . . agreed to go through with this."

"The other part is because you think Matt is a gorgeous, sexy hunk and you've fallen in love with him, even if you haven't realized it yet," Kristina said bluntly.

Kayla arched her eyebrows. "When did you become an incurable romantic?"

"On the night I arrived in Philadelphia and Boyd took me in his arms and told me that we were never going to be separated again. The same night you met Matt Minteer. It was a magical night for us both, Kayla."

"Everything that has happened since was the result of that one night," Kayla murmured quizzically. It had been, perhaps, the most fateful night of her life.

And tonight was another—her wedding night. Kayla was more than a little apprehensive as she and Matt left the tavern among shouts and handfuls of rice from the well-wishers. She sat beside him in the front seat of his car, feeling awkward and shy.

It was so much easier to talk to him when she was angry. She had no trouble thinking of what to say to him then! When had she stopped feeling that consuming anger and outrage? she wondered. Probably when she had realized that marrying him had been her own choice. She'd ceased feeling like a victim of manipulation. It was important for her to feel in control; she could cope with anything as long as she believed she was. Kayla smiled wryly at the insight.

Matt caught a glimpse of her from the corner of his eye. He'd been watching her all day, gauging her reactions and responses from those first shocked moments when she'd realized that today was to be their wedding day, to now, when they were finally alone, the ceremony and his family behind them.

They hadn't had a chance to talk alone together since those tense moments in his old room when she had furiously lit into him. He admitted to himself that he'd arranged it that way.

But now here they were, married, and he was ridiculously uncertain what to say to his own wife. He cleared his throat. "Why are you smiling?" he asked bluntly, too bluntly, and he nearly groaned at his lack of finesse. Trying again, he plastered what he hoped would appear to be a friendly, inviting smile on his face and asked, "Care to share the joke?"

"According to your brother Luke, the joke is on you. He accused me of deliberately plotting to get pregnant so you would have to marry me. He sees you as the victim of my nefarious scheme."

"Well, we both know Luke is wrong. I'm sorry if he said anything to upset you. I'll set him straight about us as soon as I can."

Kayla shrugged. "You don't have to. It's none of his business, anyway."

"But I don't want him to think that—"

"You fell for the oldest trick in the book?" Kayla asked dryly. "I guess it's something of a blow to your ego to have your brother believe that."

"I was going to say that I don't want Luke thinking that my wife is a nefarious schemer," corrected Matt. "I know you're accustomed to putting words in other people's mouths—it's what you do for a living—but kindly let me speak for myself."

"Oh, yes, sir!" She gave him a mock salute.

He cast her a quick, curious glance. "Do you mind if I ask you something?"

"You can ask, but I might not answer. Or if I do, you might not like the answer," she finished coolly.

"Okay. Are you still angry at me? And if you are, how angry are you?"

Her cool instantly evaporated. "You expect me to gauge my anger? Like an earthquake on the Richter scale?"

"I was simply trying to determine how things stand between us, Kayla. This is our wedding night and—"

"Oh, I get it. You were trying to figure out if you were going to score tonight!"

"Score? I haven't thought in those terms since my college days. Give me a little credit, Kayla. Anyway, we're married. A husband doesn't *score* with his own wife."

"That's certainly going to be true in your case."

"You're telling me you won't sleep with me tonight? Is that it?"

"That's right. Not only are we going to have separate beds, I intend to sleep in a separate room." She stopped suddenly and turned to him. "Where are we going anyway?"

He hadn't mentioned a destination and until now, she hadn't asked about one. They were on a dark road, heading into the mountains, the lights from the city glowing in the distance behind them. There were no other cars to be seen.

"It's a surprise."

She decided his smile was distinctly menacing. Kayla shivered, but characteristically decided to tough it out. "You'd better not try to take me on some primitive camping trip in the woods," she warned. "Because I categorically refuse to camp."

"Is that so?"

"Yes!"

He laughed wickedly. "Then you're really in for a surprise, Mrs. Minteer." He turned the car onto a two-lane road leading higher into the mountains, deeper into the woods. Not even the faintest glimmer of the city lights could be seen in the rearview mirror now.

He was actually going to do it! Kayla thought wildly. He intended to camp out on his wedding night! In these cold mountains in the middle of March! "Take me back to Johnstown right now," she commanded.

Matt kept right on grinning and didn't bother to reply. He didn't turn the car around and head back toward Johnstown, either.

"It's too cold to spend the night in a tent in the middle of a forest in the mountains. Furthermore, if I get sick, it won't be good for the baby," she added righteously.

"Who said anything about a tent? Tents are for wimps. I like putting the old sleeping bags on top of a pile of leaves and sleeping right under the stars." He shot her a sidelong glance. "And I hope you don't intend to use the baby as an excuse to get your way for the next eight months."

"You're an insensitive bully!" Kayla stormed. "No force on earth is strong enough to make me sleep on a pile of leaves! I'll spend the night in the car. And—" She stopped speaking abruptly.

Matt had pulled the car onto a brightly lit roadway that had suddenly appeared, as if out of nowhere. A stone lodge stood at the center of a wide circular driveway. A hand-lettered sign hanging on a post read, Keystone Inn.

"You were saying?" Matt prompted. "Something about spending the night in the car?" He braked to a stop in front of the building. "I myself am going inside. I have reservations here." He opened the car door.

"You—you—" she spluttered. "You deliberately let me think—"

"I plead guilty to the charges." Matt was laughing. "You were so insistent, so indignant, so irate. I had to do it, I couldn't help myself."

Kayla's lips quivered. In another moment, she was laughing, too. "I'm still irate, you snake! Do you know how scared I was? Sleeping on a pile of leaves, outside, in thirty-five-degree weather?"

The prospect, which moments before had outraged her, now seemed so ridiculous she laughed even harder. "You're a fiend!'' She reached over to sock him. He swiftly moved out of her reach.

"Let me put your mind at ease, Kayla." He was still laughing. "I hate camping, probably more than you do. I wouldn't do it if I were paid to. I associate all those trees and forest flora in the great outdoors with massive sinus headaches. I have allergies," he explained. "All the Minteers do. Chances are the baby will, too. We can vacation at the beach, away from trees, grass and greenery."

He got out of the car. Kayla opened her door and was getting out when he appeared at her side to assist her. They stood together, facing each other outside the car. Both were still chuckling at his successful joke.

Their eyes met and they stared at each other, their laughter fading. Kayla gazed into his thickly-lashed dark blue eyes and suddenly felt shaky and breathless and wildly, excitingly aware of everything around her—the cool, fresh scent of the mountain air, the tree branches crackling in the breeze, the warmth emanating from Matt's tall, strong frame so very close to her.

"Forgive me?" Matt asked softly. His eyes flickered to her mouth. Her lips were full and beautifully shaped. He remembered their softness, their taste, and a sweetly sharp pain of arousal stabbed him. "I teased you. I shouldn't have."

Kayla swayed toward him. "I deserved it. I did sound awfully—uh—imperious."

His hands went to her waist. "As overbearing and dogmatic as you accuse me of being." He lowered his head and touched his lips to hers, a kiss that was much too brief to be satisfying. "I told you we were a good match. I need someone strong enough to stand up to me when I'm on my high horse. And you need someone you can't run all over."

"It sounds more like the clash of the titans instead of a marriage." She went up on tiptoe and wrapped her arms around his neck. At that moment, she realized how much she wanted him to be right, how much she wanted to believe their enforced marriage really could work.

Matt responded instantly to her unspoken plea. His arms went tightly around her and he lifted her up against the hard breadth of his body as his mouth claimed hers for a deep, hungry kiss.

Soon, too soon for either of them, he released her. Kayla's feet were back on solid ground once more, but her head was in the clouds. Matt took her hand and they walked inside in a silence laden with anticipation and arousal.

A huge mahogany desk ran the length of one wall of the inn and a big brick fireplace dominated the other wall where a fire crackled brightly behind the screened grate. An assortment of comfortable-looking couches and chairs were strategically placed, with the fireplace as the focus, giving the lounge a cozily inviting air.

"It's lovely," Kayla exclaimed.

Matt smiled. "We're near several ski resorts, but this place draws a clientele that prefers a more quiet and private atmosphere off the slopes. It's usually booked far in advance, but since there hasn't been much snow this winter we were able to get a last-minute reservation."

She could have asked him when the reservations were made—undoubtedly *before* he'd bothered to consult her about marrying her—but Kayla didn't feel like starting another argument. In truth, the last thing she was feeling was argumentative.

As she and Matt entered their room—a charmingly decorated suite boasting a canopied bed and an enormous clawfoot antique bathtub—she felt romantic and sexy and excited. And enormously touched that Matt had arranged to have their wedding night in a special, romantic place.

"Look what we have here." Matt was tugging the cellophane from a wide basket filled with fresh fruit, cheeses, small tins of crackers and cookies, and a sleek gold box of chocolates. "Are you hungry?"

"After all that food at the reception?"

Matt smiled. "There was a lot of food but I didn't see you eating much of it. You've got to be hungry. After all, you're eating for two, remember?"

Kayla groaned at the cliché, but the food in the basket did look tempting. "Actually, I am feeling kind of hungry. This is the first time all day that my stomach hasn't been tied in a knot."

She surprised herself. She *was* relaxed with Matt. Usually, she felt tense and edgy.

"There's a bottle of champagne," Matt said, opening the small refrigerator in a corner of the room. "That's off-limits for you, in your condition, though. I'll call the desk and ask them to send up some ginger ale."

"Thank you. That's very thoughtful of you." Kayla swallowed. "It was also thoughtful of you to get this room for tonight. I mean, it would have been practical and convenient for us to have spent the night in your duplex in Johnstown, but—"

"You're my bride, Kayla, and this is our wedding night. I didn't want it to be practical and convenient."

She smiled softly. "You have a romantic streak." The knowledge warmed her.

"If I do, you're the only one who's ever brought it out," Matt said wryly. He thought briefly of Debra who'd found him the epitome of all that was practical, convenient and controlled. Kayla brought forth facets of him he'd never known were there. And instead of being alarmed by it, he felt pleased.

After they'd eaten and drunk their fill, his romantic streak surfaced again, when he picked her up in his arms and carried her into the bedroom. He laid her carefully on the bed and then came down beside her, taking her in his arms and kissing her with possessive hunger. She was his bride, his wife, the mother of his unborn child. An intense wave of protective tenderness surged through him, combining irrevocably with the passion she evoked.

"You make me feel things no other woman ever has," he confessed huskily. He molded her to the long, hard length of his body, making her achingly aware of his ardent male need. All rational thought was swiftly receding under the urgent onslaught of passion and emotion.

Kayla gazed up at him with wide, limpid eyes. She felt weak and soft and hot, completely pliant beneath his hands. The pleasure he so expertly gave her rendered her mindless and she luxuriated in the pure sensuality of their kisses and caresses.

Swiftly, they dispensed with their clothing, offering each other assistance when needed, sharing an intimacy that seemed seductively familiar, without any awkwardness or inhibitions. They were perfectly attuned to each other, united in an erotic rhythm that was both age-old and distinctively, uniquely their own.

"Oh, Matt, now, please now!" she said throatily. Her impassioned cry was both a surrender and command, and Matt was eager to accept both.

"Yes, baby. Yes, love." His body came down heavily on hers and their eyes, intense and revealing, met.

Their gazes locked, Matt surged powerfully into her and Kayla took him deeply inside, forging the bonds between them into a complex union of physical and emotional needs and desires.

And together they savored every moment, every nuance, every thrill until their passion reached flash point and burst into an intense, shattering climax, simultaneously thrusting them to the heights of rapture. They lingered there in brilliant timeless bliss before drifting slowly down into the warm sensuous seas of satisfaction.

"I wish we could've stayed longer at the inn," Matt said wistfully as he inserted his key in the door of his apartment. It was shortly before two p.m.; they'd checked out of the inn late that morning to drive to Harrisburg. "Unfortunately, the legislature is in session tomorrow and we have a vote on a bill that the governor has been pushing since his election."

He opened the door and ushered her inside. "Well, this is it. My official Harrisburg residence."

Kayla took in the combined living-dining room with the miniscule kitchen tucked into a corner. The area was furnished with a huge beanbag chair, doubtless a relic from somebody's college days, a television set and a folding chair in front of a snack tray. It was possible to look into the small bedroom and bath when standing here at the front door. "You actually live here?" she asked incredulously.

"I—uh—guess it is a bit primitive," he admitted, seeing the place through her eyes. "But since the legislature is only in session Monday through Wednesday, everybody usually goes back to their home districts for the rest of the week. I have the duplex in Johnstown and I didn't want to spend a fortune on a place here."

"Well, if it suits you . . ." Kayla's voice trailed off. She didn't know how it could. Even three days a week in this dump was three too many.

"I do have a brand-new mattress on the bed," Matt offered. "It's the best piece of furniture I own."

"I think I remember you mentioning that at one time." She cast a quick, nervous glance at her watch. "Matt, I really should be heading back to Washington. I have some things I'd like to get done before Monday mor—"

"Back to Washington?" Matt interrupted, frowning. "But we were married yesterday! Should I remind you that it's traditional for husbands and wives to live together?"

"Live where?" Kayla felt a quiver of anxiety leap and grow within her. "You commute back and forth between Harrisburg and Johnstown. My home and my office is in

Washington.'' She gulped. ''This is something we should have discussed and settled long before we married.''

''There wasn't time. Anyway, it's not a problem. You're my wife and you'll live with me, Kayla. You may as well give up your apartment. After the election we'll have to live in D.C., but we'll need a bigger place with the baby and all.''

She gaped at him. ''Let me see if I get this straight. According to you, I should simply close my office, move out of my apartment and into this . . . this dump?''

''We'll find a bigger place, a nicer place, as soon as possible,'' he cut in quickly. ''We'll start looking tomorrow if you want. And next weekend, we can rent a trailer and move your furniture up here. You have much better-looking stuff than I do,'' he conceded.

''That's the only point you've made that I agree with.'' She cast a disdainful look around the room. *A green velour beanbag chair big enough to seat three?* But even that visual assault paled when compared to the bombshell he'd just dropped. ''Matt, I can't simply quit my business. I have clients who've hired me, I can't just drop them.''

She braced herself for the explosion she was certain would follow. The prospect of quarreling with him again left her gloomy and dispirited. They hadn't exchanged a cross word since their arrival at the Keystone Inn. On the contrary, they had been particularly close and compatible in every way, right up until they'd entered this hole-in-the-wall that served as his apartment.

She didn't want it to end, not the closeness, not the affection, not the sex. Tears stung her eyes.

Matt heaved a sigh. ''You're right. You can't drop them cold.''

Her head jerked up and she stared at him, almost giddy with relief that the dreaded argument wasn't going to occur after all. ''Oh, Matt, I—''

''I know you have to give them some sort of notice.'' He caught her hand and pulled her to him, wrapping his arms around her. "But, dammit, Kayla, I hate the thought of being away from you. I want you with me. All the time," he added, his voice husky and impassioned.

According to Penny and a slew of philosophical tracts, wasn't this the time to launch into a lecture about her rights and responsibilities to her career? Kayla knew it was, but the words wouldn't come. She found his need for her enthralling, his desire to have her with him nearly irresistible.

Had there ever been a time in her life when she'd been wanted and needed by anyone except her twin? Maybe while her mother was still alive, but that was twenty-one long years ago. Their father had panicked at the thought of raising his daughters alone, had quickly remarried, then conveniently died to escape them all, and Penny had taken a turn at being stuck with them. Certainly, Scott Ceres, her first and only lover, hadn't found the idea of permanence with a McClure appealing; he'd opted for media wizard Dillon's daughter Victoria instead.

But Matt had married *her* and not, it seemed, in name only. He wanted a real marriage, a wife who shared his home and his life. He wanted her, Kayla McClure... Minteer.

"I want to be with you, too, Matt," Kayla dared to admit. She drew back a little and gazed up at him with shining, serious eyes. "I understand that if it's going to work between us, things will have to change."

Kayla was astonished at just how willing she was to make those changes. "I'll tell my clients that I'm married and expecting a baby and will be living away from Washington for a while. But if any of them choose to retain me, I'd like to continue acting as a consultant."

"I don't want you flying all over the place on behalf of your clients. I don't want you spending too much time on them or with them. I want your first priorities to be our marriage and our child."

"I just told you they are," she said impatiently. "Realistically speaking, do you think many politicians are going to stick with a consultant who puts them last, after her husband and family and his career? You're a politician. You know anybody working for one had better be willing to put everything and everybody else well after their boss's political career."

Matt's blue eyes pierced her. "Would you do it? Put your husband and family and my career ahead of your clients?"

"One thing I won't do is to be the stereotypical politician's wife," she countered fiercely. "I've observed their position up close, you know. I've seen the politician's staff shunt the wife aside as an annoyance to them and a distraction to their boss. I've even done it myself, I'm sorry to admit."

"I wouldn't let that happen to you!" Matt protested.

"I won't let it happen to me, either," retorted Kayla. "I'm going to take your career as seriously as I've taken any I've been hired to help work on. I'm going to share your life as your full partner, not your dependent spouse. And if that means giving you advice or arguing with your staff, so be it. I know your brother Luke is your closest adviser, but he is not going to relegate me to the sidelines of your career and your life."

"I'd like to see him try," Matt said dryly. His eyes held hers as he reached out and caught hold of her wrist. "But let's get one thing straight, Kayla. You're my wife, *not* my political handler."

His voice echoed his distaste for the very words. He pulled her toward him, his compelling dark blue eyes as forceful and binding as his hand that manacled her wrist.

"You'll take wifely advice but not professional advice, is that what you're saying?" She sensed the controlled desire in him and it drew her like a magnet. She wanted to unleash that desire, to make him lose that steely cool control. She was very good at that, she congratulated herself with warm feminine satisfaction. Smiling seductively, she took a step closer to him, then another.

"I'm telling you that I—" Matt's voice faltered as she slipped her hands under his sweater.

"Go on," she encouraged, leaning into him as her fingers stroked sensual patterns on the warm skin of his chest.

Matt spread his thighs and anchored her between them, his palms cupping the firm curves of her buttocks. He knew what she was wearing under her jeans—brief aqua bikini panties that matched her lacy bra. He'd watched her put them on this morning after he had dried her with the fluffy white towel provided by the inn.

Heat flashed through him at the very intimate memory. He pictured the two of them as they had been earlier that morning, in that ridiculously big bathtub where they had made some more sizzlingly erotic memories.

"You were saying," Kayla prompted, softly nuzzling his neck. She shivered as a tingling liquid warmth coiled inside her.

"I don't remember," he mumbled. "And I don't care." He caught her face between his hands and kissed her with a passion mixed with yearning need. "Stay with me, Kayla. Don't leave me."

His consuming need for her was as enveloping and alluring as his pure masculine hunger. "I'm not going anywhere," Kayla promised, lifting her lips for his kiss. She knew at that moment that she loved him. Those four *D*'s—the distrust, disbelief, disappointment and disillusionment—that Penny had instilled in her, the strictures which had governed her life, were submerged by a rush of emotions and one powerful insight.

That love was definitely a risk worth taking.

Eleven

***

"**K**ayla! This is a surprise!" Elena Teslovic greeted Kayla on Monday morning as she walked into the rented store-front room in downtown Harrisburg where Teslovic supporters gathered to work on their candidate's upcoming campaign. "I didn't know you were going to be in town to-day."

"As it turns out, I'll be spending most of my time in Harrisburg—at least until after the November election," Kayla said, smiling softly. "You see, over the weekend I—"

"I'm so glad you're here so I can tell you the news in person," Elena interrupted excitedly. "I got the strangest phone call earlier today with the most astonishing news. We spent half the morning tracking sources, to see if it's true. And it is!"

"What's that, Elena?" Kayla asked. She wasn't miffed that Elena wasn't interested in hearing about her weekend; she was well versed in the ways of candidates. Nothing captured and held their interest as much as their own unfolding campaigns.

"Dave Wilson isn't going to run for reelection. He doesn't even want his name on the primary ballot. He's conceding the field to me!" Elena exclaimed. "Now there is nobody planning to run against me."

Kayla's jaw dropped. "What happened? I can't even hazard a guess. I never thought he would simply quit."

"*You* happened, Kayla!" Elena cried exuberantly. "I'm convinced you're the reason he's quitting. Rumors were flying that I'd hired a big-city consultant from D.C. and Wilson just panicked. He supposedly admitted that his reputation couldn't withstand the kind of mud-slinging media attack he knew Dillon and Ward was capable of designing. So he pulled out of the race!"

"But I'm not working for that agency anymore," Kayla protested.

"Of course, *we* know that, but you know how rumors are and how quickly they spread. Obviously, the fact that you *used* to work for Dillon and Ward was amended to your currently working there." Elena grinned gleefully. "No wonder Wilson quit. Dillon and Ward would've done a first-rate hatchet job on him. He had no way of knowing we were going to take a more honorable course, simply by letting his abysmal record speak for itself."

"We would've nailed him," an aide added loyally.

"So as of now, I guess I'm no longer a client, Kayla," Elena said ruefully. "I'd love to keep you on but you know how tight my campaign budget is."

"I know. And I wish you the best of luck with your campaign and your career, Elena," Kayla said warmly, offering her hand to shake. "Even if you're not my client, I hope you'll be my friend."

"You can count on that," Elena promised effusively. "Oh, and Kayla, you might as well take this." She handed her a fat folder, crammed with sheaths of paper. "Maybe you can use some of this material sometime."

"Elena, you have three calls on hold," said a staffer, and Kayla knew it was time to leave. There was no place for a non-worker in a campaign headquarters and she was no longer involved in plotting the course of Elena's political destiny.

An hour later, as arranged earlier that morning, she met Kristina for lunch at Rillo's. Her sister was sitting at the table when Kayla arrived with her incredible news about Wilson's decision to drop out.

Kristina laughed at the idea of her twin as a specter of political doom, terrifying and powerful enough to overwhelm the opposition without even taking a poll.

And then: "I submitted my resignation to PITA last week, Kayla." Kristina's hazel eyes were suddenly misty. "I'm working the rest of this week and then I'm packing up and moving to Atlanta. Boyd and I would like a traditional June wedding with all the trimmings—or at least most of them—so I'll have a few months to plan for it and look for a new job there."

"Atlanta," Kayla repeated slowly. "It's so far away."

"Hey, that's my line." Kristina grinned. "You're supposed to tell me how close we'll be by air and by phone. It's true too, Kayla. You know we'll talk and visit often."

"I know. But it seems ironic that I'll be in Harrisburg, at least until Matt wins the election—if he wins—and takes office in D.C., and you won't be here."

"You're going to be living here with Matt? I was sure you would insist on staying by yourself at your place in D.C. and I was just as certain he wouldn't go for the idea."

"I called Jolene this morning and told her to reschedule any appointments to Thursday and Friday. Matt will be finished for the week and can come to Washington with me.

I'm not sure about the agency's future...I do know I'm going to put my family first.''

Kristina heaved a relieved sigh. ''Now I guess I won't need to give you the speech I've been preparing. The one about compromise and sacrifice and pulling out all stops for love.''

''I think I gave myself that same speech yesterday,'' Kayla said with a small, reminiscent smile. Her eyes widened, as an idea suddenly struck. ''Kristina, if you're leaving town at the end of the week, would you sublet your place to Matt and me? One of our compromises is to find another apartment in Harrisburg for the time we'll be living here. If you saw Matt's current place, you'd understand why.''

Kristina quickly agreed to the sublet, and the sisters were talking furnishings when a shadow fell over the table. They simultaneously looked up to see Luke Minteer standing above them.

'''Double, double, toil and trouble, fire burn, and cauldron bubble,''' he quoted flatly. ''What are you witches plotting now?'' Missing was the playful smile and teasing gleam in his eyes that would've couched his words in humor instead of insult.

Kayla grimaced. Luke had declared war on her on her wedding day, but she didn't expect continuing open hostility from him. She decided to try to tactfully deflect him. ''If that's a joke, I don't appreciate it, Luke.'' But her flashing eyes belied her light tone.

''And I don't appreciate your wrecking my brother's career,'' Luke shot back.

''What are you talking about?'' Kristina asked coldly. ''She's done nothing of the sort.''

Luke grabbed an unoccupied chair, pulled it over and sat down at their table. ''Dave Wilson announced this morning that he isn't seeking reelection to his state seat. He was spooked by reports that his competitor had hired a cut-throat, down-and-dirty political consultant and so he decided to throw in the towel and withdraw from the race. One guess who that political consultant might be?"

"I know," said Kayla evenly. "Me. And he credited me with a cut-throat, down-and-dirty reputation that I haven't earned." She eyed him curiously. "Are you upset because Wilson withdrew in favor of Elena? The man is sleazy and sneaky and thoroughly reprehensible, the sort that gives all politicians a bad name. It's a blessing he's leaving office."

"He's leaving his *state* office," Luke corrected. "And it's no blessing, because he's decided to run for federal office. Wilson sent out a later announcement that he now intends to run for the same U.S. House seat that Matt is seeking."

"He can't do that!" Kristina said indignantly.

"Unfortunately, he can," Luke snapped. "His district and Matt's comprise the same area for the congressional seat, so he's eligible. In a typical Wilson back-stabbing double-cross, he is taking back his support of Matt on the grounds that he himself is better equipped to 'handle the increased responsibilities of national office' was the way he phrased it."

"He's running against Matt?" Kayla repeated, floored by the news. "The man is daft as well as corrupt. He doesn't stand a chance."

"He most certainly does," Luke said coldly. "Wilson's staff is a highly effective propaganda machine. How do you think he's held his state office for so long? Everybody in government knows what a lying louse the man is, but he's managed to ingratiate himself with the voters. And then there's this!" He tossed a large manila envelope onto the table. "Take a look, Kayla. The remains of Matt's career are inside."

Silently, with trembling fingers, Kayla reached into the envelope and removed several photographs, 8x10 glossies of herself sitting on Matt's lap at the fund-raiser that fateful night they'd met. Both of them looked giddy and decidedly sexually hungry for each other. To a stranger viewing the photos, Matt would appear to be a boozing womanizer, she, one of those ubiquitous party girls making her rounds.

It was not a portrait of a future U.S. congressman and his wife.

Kristina was looking over her shoulder. "Oh, damn!" she breathed.

"My sentiments exactly," said Luke caustically. "The little scheme you two dreamed up to land a husband has boomeranged, hasn't it? As Mrs. Minteer, Kayla, your future is bound up in Matt's success, which you've just sabotaged."

"That's a hateful thing to say!" Kristina exclaimed furiously. "Not to mention completely untrue."

Luke ignored her. His attention was focused on Kayla, his blue eyes glittering. "I've learned from reliable sources that if Matt doesn't drop out of the race, Wilson is going public about the fund-raiser. He plans to release these pictures to his hometown newspaper, anonymously, of course. Except in his version of events, the waiters were instructed to spike the beverages and food to put the guests in a more, shall we say generous, frame of mind and beef up campaign contributions."

"But that's a bald-faced lie!" cried Kayla.

"There is no one around from WINDS left to repute it," Luke countered, not bothering to add that he had been instrumental in running them out of the state to parts unknown. "So what we have is Wilson's allegations of a drunken brawl, with the candidate cuddling a sexy little broad on his lap in full view of everyone, and pictures to support his claim. Believe me, knowledge of elected officials indulging in wild parties and cavorting with hot sexy babes might be acceptable to voters in certain other states but *not* here in western Pennsylvania."

"My sister is not a hot sexy babe," Kristina muttered, but most of the fire was gone from her voice. When faced with it, she recognized a potential scandal and its probable outcome. "Oh, Kayla, this is awful!"

Awful was too mild a word, Kayla thought grimly. "Does Matt know?" she asked Luke anxiously.

Luke scowled. "Of course he knows. I told him the moment I heard. He wasn't happy about it, I can tell you that."

Kayla quickly rose to her feet. "Where is he? In his office? I want to see him."

"He has a luncheon meeting and then an afternoon session in the legislature," Luke told her. "And I'd advise you to stay away from his office. You're unlikely to receive a warm welcome from *anyone* if you make the mistake of going there."

Kayla felt a sharp swift stab of pain, psychological in origin but almost physical in intensity. She was well aware of Matt's opinion of political handlers, and now the presence of one—her!—had resulted in an inadvertent shake-up that was already causing reverberations in his own future.

"Unless you're hell-bent on destroying any chances Matt has, you'll make yourself scarce until we've had a chance to assess our options and define our strategy," Luke said harshly. "Go back to Washington and practise your skulduggery there. We don't want or need you here!"

It sounded so much like something Matt himself might say. Had already said? Kayla tried to swallow around the sudden lump that tightened her throat. She watched Luke snatch the photos and shove them back into the envelope with barely concealed fury. He stalked off without another word, leaving the twins sitting stunned and bereft at their table.

"He had no right to speak to you that way," Kristina wailed. "And to imply that you're somehow at fault for this mess is as vicious and malicious as anything that scoundrel Dave Wilson could ever say."

"Do you think Luke's speaking for Matt?" Kayla whispered. "Delivering a message from him?"

That possibility had also occurred to Kristina. Kayla could see it in her eyes.

"I—I don't want to believe that, Kayla," Kristina said sadly. "Not two days after your wedding."

"My wedding," Kayla echoed. "Despite the traditional trappings and the presence of all the Minteers and their good wishes, it was still, ultimately, a shotgun wedding, Kristina. Damage control, as we in the business say."

And despite Matt's insistence to the contrary, a wedding resulting from political damage control rather than true love, did not portend a lasting, loving marriage. The sisters gazed at each other, as the potent forces of distrust, disbelief, disappointment and disillusionment swept over them in overlapping waves.

"You can't say Penny didn't prepare us for something like this," Kristina said glumly. "She's always encouraged us to brace ourselves for probable misery. I called her yesterday to tell her about your wedding, by the way."

"Let me guess—she said the marriage would never last," Kayla intoned flatly, taking a bolstering sip of ice water. "But things are falling apart at a rate that would surprise even Penny."

"She's sending you a wedding card with a check made out only to you," Kristina said, sighing. "Says you're going to need every cent you can get to support yourself and a child. No mention was made of Matt, of course, because she doesn't believe he'll be around long."

As Kayla headed back to Matt's tiny apartment to get her things, she sadly acknowledged that she shared Penny's dark view. She didn't believe Matt would be around long, either, not after Luke's news.

She steadfastly blinked back the rush of tears that filled her eyes. Crying was useless; control was everything. She needed to remember that.

Kayla numbly tossed her clothes into her suitcase. She'd certainly done a lot of packing these past few days. She remembered her swift and sleepy packing job Saturday morning, when she'd scarcely been awake. She'd had no idea of the plans Matt had made for later that day—plans for their wedding!

She had been in an altogether different frame of mind yesterday when she'd repacked at the Keystone Inn after their wedding night. A heated flush warmed her as a kaleidoscope of memories shifted before her mind's eye: sensual scenes of her and Matt passionately making love and then lying in each other's arms afterward, talking softly, even laughing together in intimate camaraderie. She'd been so happy, more confident and optimistic about the future than she had ever been in her life.

For better or for worse. The words from the marriage vows she'd taken suddenly resounded in her ears. Kayla inhaled on a sob. Yesterday had been "for better." Who would have guessed that the "for worse" would occur so heartbreakingly soon?

But it had. Kayla snapped her suitcase shut. And now she was leaving. Being run out of town, actually. She frowned, picked up the case and walked to the door. She paused, her hand on the knob.

After two days of marriage she was leaving her husband? Why, even Penny's marriages lasted longer than that! Something deep inside her seemed to snap.

"There are two paths you can follow and the choice is yours." That was the standard opening statement she made to her clients. *"One leads to winning, the other to losing."* She would always urge them to choose the winning path, even though it invariably meant there would be obstacles to overcome. Ironically, she was about to choose the losing path for herself, to give up without even trying.

Kayla set down her suitcase. "I'm not going," she said aloud. Just the sound of her own voice strengthened her resolve. Hadn't she already decided that she was going to *work* at making her marriage succeed? She knew what work involved: staying power, making an effort, accepting a challenge, trying different approaches until achieving success.

She was good at working at her career, but she'd never applied all her energies and instincts and strengths to her personal life. She fought for her clients all the time, but she'd never fought on her own behalf. She had quietly ceded Scott Ceres to Victoria Dillon with nary a protesting word. Because she hadn't cared enough to fight for him?

Kayla frowned thoughtfully. Whatever had happened in the past for whatever reason, things were totally different when it came to Matt. She loved him. She was going to fight for him and work for him and salvage his career and their marriage.

She sank down into the enormous beanbag chair and opened the folder that Elena had returned to her. Being enveloped in the cushiony softness was surprisingly comfortable. Maybe she wouldn't insist on pitching out the giant beanbag when they moved into Kristina's place. *If* they did . . .

Kayla determinedly squelched that negative thought, uncapped her pen, pulled out a stack of papers and went to work.

An hour later, she was so deeply absorbed in her task that she didn't hear the door open, didn't see Matt standing on the threshold.

"You're still here." His deep voice, low and urgent, resounded through the room.

Kayla gave a startled little gasp and dropped her pen. "Matt!" She stood up quickly and the papers went flying all over the floor. "I—wasn't expecting you," she said breathlessly. "I'd planned to go to your office later this afternoon, after today's session was adjourned. I guess I lost track of the time."

She stared at him, standing there in his dark suit, looking so vital and vibrantly male. Her pulse began to race. His blue eyes were glittering, his expression as serious and intense as usual. But she couldn't for the life of her tell whether he was glad she was still here... or not.

Her heart in her throat, she took a hesitant step toward him. "Matt, I talked to Luke today and—"

"I know," Matt interrupted, striding toward her. "I just talked to him myself. I went directly to my office from the senate floor and my idiot brother told me that he'd seen you earlier."

Idiot brother? That sounded promising, but she wasn't assuming anything. "Matt, I'm sorry Dave Wilson double-crossed you and I know how shocked you must be but—"

"Dave Wilson is the biggest double-crossing backstabber in Harrisburg. I'm never shocked when he acts in character." Matt stopped to stand directly in front of her. "What did shock me was that my own brother told me he blamed *you* for Wilson's actions. That he told you to get lost. I could only imagine how you'd react to that!" His fingers curved around her upper arms. "I rushed back here, expecting to find you gone."

Her lips twisted into a small, nervous smile. "Well, I'm still here. Are you angry or—" she swallowed "—relieved?"

"Ah, Kayla, how can you even ask me that?" He pulled her roughly into his arms.

Kayla felt a wild impulse to burst into tears and laugh out loud, both at the same time. "How could I not ask?" she whispered hoarsely. "Luke does have a valid point in that none of this—from Wilson's quitting the race against Elena to his threatening to use those pictures of us—would've happened if I didn't exist."

He brushed his mouth against her ear. "I'm damn glad that you do exist, Kayla. And that we found each other, no matter how unorthodox our meeting was. I'm even gladder that we skipped all those stupid prerequisite dating rituals and jumped directly into marriage. Dating is make-believe and marriage is real life and I've always opted for reality over fantasy."

She clung to him, staring up at him with tear-jeweled eyes, wanting to believe him with all her heart. Finding that she was beginning to believe him. "But what about the campaign?" she had to ask.

He shrugged impatiently. "What about it? I'll run and win. I don't know why Luke is so hyper. Now let's forget about politics and everybody connected with it and concentrate on us."

He cupped the nape of her neck with one hand and pressed his other hand against the small of her back, locking her to him as he clamped his mouth possessively, passionately over hers.

Their mutual desire and the fierce emotional tension served as a lightning rod for the passion that flared between them. They never made it as far as the bedroom. Hastily discarding the clothes they impatiently tore off themselves and each other, Kayla and Matt sank into the inviting, enveloping comfort of the big beanbag chair.

Eager and ready, they merged, rocking with a driving sensuous rhythm that consumed them both. The pleasure was so intense that they tried to prolong it, wanting it to go on and on, but inevitably, the white-hot firestorm reached its apex, bursting into a brilliant, rapturous release.

They lay together in a blissful languor for a long time, cocooned in the sweet afterglow of fulfillment. The giant beanbag complied to their contours. Kayla ran her hand over the dark velour cover. "When I first saw this thing, I thought it was the most hideous piece of junk I'd ever laid eyes on."

"That seems to be a fairly common reaction," Matt murmured, running his hand over the silky skin of her stomach.

"But I've changed my mind. Now I think we'll have to take it with us, wherever we end up living."

"You know where we're going to live, baby. After I win the election in November, we'll divide our time between Washington and Johnstown."

"You're not at all worried about Dave Wilson running against you in the primary? Matt, he has those pictures of us. And Luke said he was going to lie about what really happened at the fund-raiser."

"I saw the pictures. Big deal. We look like a couple who happen to be madly in love with each other. The fact that we were married six weeks later confirms it."

"A couple in love?" Kayla said softly. She had viewed the pictures through the perspective of a political consultant and had seen them as damning; Matt saw them in an entirely different light.

"Which we were," he added firmly. "We just didn't realize it yet. And we are. In love, that is. I know it, even if you don't."

She went very still. "You love me?" she whispered.

"I love you." His straightforward declaration was pure Matt.

"Oh, Matt, I love you, too!" she cried, hugging him with all her might, her heart shining in her eyes. "And I was so afraid that it was going to be over before we really had a chance because Wilson—"

Matt made an exclamation of disbelief. "The day I let a twit like Wilson break up my marriage will be the day..." He paused, searching for a suitable analogy. And gave up the literary struggle. "Well, it'll never happen, Kayla. We're together forever. Don't ever forget that."

"I won't," she said, twining her arms around his neck to kiss him with all the love and passion she possessed.

It was a long time before they resumed their political discussion and when they did, they were dressed and eating Mexican take-out food, sitting in the beanbag chair and using the snack tray as a table.

"I don't think you should discount Wilson so easily, Matt," Kayla said seriously, squirting *picante* sauce on her chicken taco. "The man is evil and will do anything he can to win, no matter how unethical. I know all about him, I have a lot of information on him gathered by Elena Teslovic's staff."

"I won't sink to his level and run a smear campaign, Kayla," Matt warned.

"You won't have to." She reached for the paper she'd been writing when Matt had arrived. "I was drawing up a plan. Here it is. We use quotes from Wilson himself along with quotes others have made about him in juxtaposition with your quotes and statements that have been made about you. We interpret and compare his voting record, which is one of the most pathetic ones I've ever seen, with yours." She smiled. "I'm assuming that yours is as honest and excellent as any I've ever seen?"

Matt laughed. "Never doubt it."

"I've outlined a few TV and radio ads and a couple of print ads, too. We'll blitz the area for two solid weeks before the primary. And I also think we should stress the Minteer family history, how you've been here for generations, how your family embodies the stick-to-it, never-say-die spirit of Johnstown after the flood. Your great-grandfather's story can be told and retold in print and on the air. Everybody warms to a local son with strong roots who is loyal to the area. Dave Wilson isn't that. He moved here twelve years ago after losing an election in Ohio."

"Ah, the old political opportunist-carpetbagger charge. Kayla, you know my feelings on manipulating the voters."

"I'm well aware of them," she retorted. "How could I not be? But how do you feel about saving the voters from the likes of a Dave Wilson? How do you feel about letting the public know the truth about you and your record and the truth about his?"

"Well, of course, I don't want Wilson to win. He's a greedy con artist who undermines people's faith in government."

"And we're going to make sure everybody in the congressional voting district knows it. The only thing that worries me is his threat to go to the press about what WINDS did at the fund-raiser."

"Don't worry about it." Matt shrugged, clearly more interested in unwrapping his burrito than in Dave Wilson's threats. "Wilson's not going to say a word about that night. The intrepid photographer who snapped our picture also took a few of ol' Dave that night. With a very young, very sexy woman who was most definitely not his long-suffering wife. If Dave wants to play dueling photos, he's going to lose. But if he doesn't mention that night, I won't, either."

"That's more than fair," Kayla said. "Because you could release that picture today and he'd be finished politically by tomorrow."

"I'd rather run a clean campaign and win honestly than rely on blackmail and scandal to take out my opponent."

"What a sound bite that would make!" Kayla sighed her admiration. "I really want to work with you to win this election, Matt. Won't you even consider letting me help?"

"Well, I do like your idea about incorporating the Minteer history into the campaign. I'd like to honor my family that way."

Kayla smiled widely. "I'll start working on a piece right away."

Matt deliberately shifted in the chair, so that she rolled next to him. He caught her and held her to him, pinning her with his arms and legs and smiling down into her eyes. "After all I've said to the contrary, I end up with my own personal political handler. It's sort of ironic, isn't it?"

"And maybe—just maybe—you're willing to admit that everyone in the field isn't an aspiring devil incarnate?" She playfully tweaked his chin.

He laughed and captured her hand. "The lady is a tough negotiator. But if you'll admit that not all politicians are as self-serving and corrupt as Dave Wilson, then I will admit that not all political consultants are in the same league as Dillon and Ward."

"Consider it done!" She slipped her leg between his and moved sinuously against him. "The art of compromise is definitely one of your strengths, Matthew Minteer."

He nuzzled her neck, molding her intimately against him with his big, strong hands. "The art of loving is another. Shall I demonstrate, Michaela?"

"Please do," she whispered, holding him, needing him, loving him for all time.

Epilogue

Eight months later, U.S. Congressman Matthew Minteer—who'd handily won the election by a landslide—arrived at his wife's hospital room with a dozen red roses in one arm and a giant pink teddy bear in the other. He smiled proudly as he strode into the room that was already well-stocked with flowers and balloons and gaily wrapped packages topped with pink ribbons.

Little Maura Kathleen Minteer lay snoozing in her mother's arms, oblivious to everything. With wide wondrous eyes Kayla gazed down at her baby daughter. When she looked up, she saw Matt watching them, his dark blue eyes possessive and proud and just a tad misty. She held out her hand to him, and he quickly laid down the roses and the bear and crossed the room to take it and kiss her fingertips.

"It's the most beautiful sight I've ever seen," he said huskily. "My wife holding our child. I want to capture it in my mind and keep it there forever."

"And as a backup, you have those three rolls of film you've taken of us since yesterday," Kayla said dryly. But her heart melted as Matt lifted baby Maura and cuddled her against his chest.

The infant opened her enormous blue eyes and gazed solemnly up at her father. Then she made a small sound that might have been a sneeze.

Matt and Kayla laughed. "The doctor said you and Maura can come home tomorrow," Matt said, sitting down on the edge of the bed. He slipped his arm around Kayla's shoulder so that he could hold both his wife and daughter. "I can't wait. It's lonely at home without you."

Six months ago, they'd bought a townhouse in a Washington subdivision loaded with young families. A nursery decorated in bright primary colors awaited its new little occupant.

Kayla leaned into him. "I can't wait to come home. I miss you."

"We're going to have company very soon. Kristina wants to come visit the moment you leave the hospital. She's crazy to see her new little niece."

Kayla grinned. "She wants me to give her a crash course on baby care, with Maura serving as the demonstrator doll. Fortunately, her baby isn't due for another eight months so she and Boyd have plenty of time to practice."

"Wait until Penny hears she's going to be a grandma again!" Matt shook his head. He'd had the pleasure of meeting his stepmother-in-law once. It had been an experience he would long remember. "Excuse me, a *step*grandmother whose former stepdaughters are far too old to be hers."

"She's quite insistent that the baby call her Penny, too," Kayla said ruefully.

"That's okay, my mom loves being called grandma." Matt brushed Kayla's silky hair with his lips. "I finished making all my phone calls to everybody in the family.

They're all thrilled to death about Maura and every one of them told me how lucky I am to have you. And how right we are for each other.''

"Everyone except Luke," Kayla guessed.

"Luke, too. He said our happiness has inspired him to marry and settle down himself. *Someday*."

"About ten years from how." Kayla laughed.

"He says more like fifteen," amended Matt.

"Well, as we both know, you can't plan these things. Fate has a way of stepping in and taking over, like it did for us."

"I'm so glad it did," Matt said fervently. He kissed her gently. "So very glad."

Kayla sighed softly, happily. "Oh, Matt, so am I."

* * * * *

Silhouette Desire

COMING NEXT MONTH

THE MAN WITH THE MIDNIGHT EYES
BJ James

Jacinda Talbot changed her life when she inherited a child.
She moved to a small town with caring neighbours. In fact,
some of the neighbours—the McLachlan men—were
almost *too* caring. . . *Almost*.

THE SILENCE OF ANGELS
Karen Keast

Katy and Connor McKellen were literally weeks away
from divorce, when Katy was called in to help an
abandoned little boy not much older than her own son
would have been if he had survived. Could a second
tragedy bring Connor and Katy back together?

JAKE'S CHRISTMAS
Elizabeth Bevarly

Jake Raglan had been to the altar once, and once was
definitely enough! Even wedding planner Rebecca Bellamy
wasn't going to be able to change his mind. Was there any
way for Rebecca to turn Xmas jingle bells into wedding
bells?

Silhouette Desire

COMING NEXT MONTH

NOT *HER* WEDDING!
Suzanne Simms

After ten long years apart Katherine St. Clair and Strong O'Kelly found out they were still married! And *then* they also discovered that their passion was red-hot. . .

BEWARE OF WIDOWS
Lass Small

Fabulous Brown Brothers

Rod Brown was told "Beware of widows bearing casseroles." But his next-door neighbour Pat Ullick was special and Rod didn't think she was a predatory female on the prowl. He thought he might enjoy it if she *was* about to set her sights on him!

IT HAD TO BE YOU
Jennifer Greene

The first time they'd kissed it had been spontaneous combustion, but Valerie had had plans that didn't include Sam Shepherd so they had parted and it had taken him a while to track he down. Now he'd found Val, he wasn't going to let her get away again—ever!

F 8463